MW00441839

Graceful Warrior - Nunnehi

ANN KIDWELL

Kimberly
Enjoy
Ann Kidwell ☺

Acknowledgements

This has been a work in progress for the last five years. One of the hardest things I have set out to do. It gave me a whole new appreciation for wordsmiths. The story came easy, the telling of it was another thing. I couldn't have done it without the following people:

First I would like to thank a couple of author friends of mine, Shanna Hatfield and Dani Harper. Shanna read my very first draft and was kind enough to go through it and explain to me many of the rules I didn't have a clue about. She did this with grace and encouragement. Dani, has been my mentor and let me bounce ideas off of her. She put things in such a way a novice could grasp.

Coworkers at my paying job have listened to me go on about my obsession with this project and read and reread many chapters. They are Kammy Hill, Jodi Stephens, June Riley and Megan Reed. Their feedback was invaluable.

Beta Readers: Robin Claytor, Kammy Hill and Ernie Chandler helped me pinpoint many mistakes and typos.

Professional Editors: Sharon Stogner and Angela McClain - tried to put the polish on my book.

Writing Class Instructor Allen Kopf amazed me with his gentle teachings and encouragement. Also, thank you to all the participants in the class that listened to my readings and offered lots of feedback. I couldn't have done it without all of you.

Excerpt

I counted four stairs as I felt my way into the cellar. I heard the door shut and the padlock locking. It was pitch black and it smelled damp, but I heard breathing and crying, then a whisper. "Where are we? What are they going to do to us? The police are never going to find me in here." Heavy sobbing and wheezing echoed in the darkness.

I felt along the wall, running my fingers across bricks and dirt. It smelled musty like wet earth. I whispered, "Keep talking and I'll try to find you. Ouch!" I fell forward over something wooden, and my palm felt a leg jerk away. "I'm sorry, I fell over something." I said.

It sounded like a little child was crying. "I'm Becca. What's your name? Is there more than one person down here? I hear someone else breathing?" My hand was next to someone's leg. They were shaking and the sobbing was coming from the person I was closest to. "I wish I could see. How long have you been down here?" I tried again to get the person to talk to me. Their voices as they whispered to each other sounded young and scared.

ANN KIDWELL

Cast of Characters

Rebecca (Becca) Nelson- 14 years old
Connie Young - 14 years old
Skye Frost - 17 years old
Luna Frost - 7 years old
Grammie – (aka Candice) Skye & Luna's Grandmother
Ryan Frost (aka Papa)
Aaron Frost - 21 years old - Skye's Cousin
Takena - Skye and Aaron's Great Grandmother - Cherokee Wise
Woman
Detective Alexandra Prosser (Alex)
Keilan
Weaver – Keilan's boss
Mason – Weaver's messenger
Mandy
Jessica - 15 years old
Tina - 15 years old
Ben Montgomery
Penny – 15 years old
Sue – 11 years old
Sabrina – 11 years old

Note: *Italicized words are used to show the thoughts of the character whose point of view is being expressed*.

ANN KIDWELL

CONTENTS

Acknowledgments i

1 Chapter One 1

2 Chapter Two 9

3 Chapter Three 17

4 Chapter Four 25

5 Chapter Five 29

6 Chapter Six 33

7 Chapter Seven 39

8 Chapter Eight 43

9 Chapter Nine 47

10 Chapter Ten 57

11 Chapter Eleven 63

12 Chapter Twelve 67

13 Chapter Thirteen 69

14 Chapter Fourteen 71

15 Chapter Fifteen 73

16 Chapter Sixteen 77

17 Chapter Seventeen 81

18 Chapter Eighteen 83

19 Chapter Nineteen 87

20	Chapter Twenty	93
21	Chapter Twenty-One	95
22	Chapter Twenty-Two	99
23	Chapter Twenty-Three	105
24	Chapter Twenty-Four	107
25	Chapter Twenty-Five	111
26	Chapter Twenty-Six	115
27	Chapter Twenty-Seven	117
28	Chapter Twenty-Eight	121
29	Chapter Twenty-Nine	125
30	Chapter Thirty	129
31	Chapter Thirty-One	137
31	Chapter Thirty-Two	139
33	Chapter Thirty-Three	143
34	Chapter Thirty-Four	147
35	Chapter Thirty-Five	149
36	Chapter Thirty-Six	151
37	Chapter Thirty-Seven	155
38	Chapter Thirty-Eight	159
39	Chapter Thirty-Nine	161
40	Chapter Forty	165
41	Chapter Forty-One	169
42	Chapter Forty-Two	171

43	Chapter Forty-Three	175
44	Chapter Forty-Four	179
45	Chapter Forty-Five	181
46	Chapter Forty-Six	183
47	Chapter Forty-Seven	187
48	Chapter Forty-Eight	191
49	Chapter Forty-Nine	195
50	Chapter Fifty	197
51	Chapter Fifty-One	199
52	Chapter Fifty-Two	201
53	Chapter Fifty-Three	203
54	Chapter Fifty-Four	207
55	Chapter Fifty-Five	209
56	Chapter Fifty-Six	211
**	Resources & Advocates	213
***	Author Page	219

Chapter One

The phone rang. Reluctantly she grabbed a towel to dry her hands.

"Hello, may I speak to Mrs. Nelson?"

"I'm Patricia Nelson."

"This is Officer Jane Yates with the Detroit Police Department, we picked-up your daughter, Rebecca, at Kmart this afternoon for shoplifting."

"What! Oh no. Let me turn down the TV... Where is she now?"

"We have her at the station, but she will be taken to the Juvenile Justice Center tonight and the Judge will see her in the morning."

"You're keeping her?"

"Yes Ma'am, she wasn't very cooperative when she was arrested. Has she done this before? I didn't see any previous arrests when I checked the database."

"No, but she seems to have changed lately. I don't know what I'm going to do with her. Was she alone?"

"No, she was with a girl named Connie Young, but from the video, she didn't seem to know that Rebecca had taken anything, so we released her. Your daughter confirmed that she didn't know."

"Officer, what did she steal, if I may ask?"

"Well, let me read you the statement she wrote:"

"I, Rebecca Nelson, shoplifted a pair of sexy black panties and a sexy black bra, by putting them in my purse."

"She wrote that?"

"Yes, Ma'am, and she appears to think it's a joke."

"I'm sorry officer; I don't know what's gotten into her. What do I need to do now?"

"She will appear before the Judge at eight o'clock tomorrow morning at the Juvenile Justice Center. She will probably be released into your custody. Here is the name and phone number of the probation officer assigned to your daughter's case. She will also be at the court and you can speak to her at that time."

"Okay, hold on officer, I need to get a pen, paper, and some tissue…." The officer could hear her blowing her nose in the background. "I'm sorry, I'm back. Would it be possible for me to speak with her?"

"One minute, hold on." The officer hands the phone to Rebecca.

"Hello."

"Hello, Becca. What were you thinking?"

"Awe, don't throw a fit, it wasn't that much."

"That's not the point, we don't steal things. If you needed something why didn't you ask me?"

"Yeah, yeah right, I know, but I didn't think you would buy me these."

"No, I wouldn't, you're only fourteen. What do you need with sexy black panties? I can't believe you did this."

"Get off my case, like you've never done nothing like this in your life."

"I haven't, and this isn't about me."

"It's always about you; Mom, everything is about you or your precious Sissy."

"Becca, where's this coming from?"

"I gotta go Mom. Go be with your precious Sissy."

The phone went dead. Hearing that grated on her nerves, as her thoughts raced. *What am I going to do? What have I done wrong? Now I have to be in Court tomorrow morning and miss a couple hours of work. Maybe I can use my sick hours so my check won't be short. Why is she doing this? I don't know how to handle her anymore. She won't listen to anything I say. She says she hates me and she is so angry all the time. Being arrested didn't even seem to bother her.*

Sissy, she's never been jealous of Sissy before. Sure they would fight as sisters do, but I never paid more attention to Sissy than I did her. Sissy's three years younger and isn't as independent as Becca, but that's all.

Maybe I should get counseling for her, but where am I going to get the money to do that? I thought I had this being a single mother thing down, now it seems to be too much for me. I can't believe Becca is in jail. If I could just quit crying, this isn't helping anything.

***

The next morning Patricia Nelson entered the crowded waiting room in the Juvenile Justice Center. A young woman standing near the reception desk called out, "Patricia Nelson, I'm looking for Patricia Nelson."

She raised her hand as she walked up to the desk. "I'm Patricia Nelson."

"Hi, I'm Karen Boles, your daughter's probation officer. They will bring Rebecca in soon, maybe within the next ten minutes. Can we talk?"

"Yes, it's nice to meet you."

Ms. Boles was messing with a pile of papers as she sat beside her on the bench and dropped her pen. *There are so many people talking, I can't think straight.* Ms. Boles placed her hand on Patricia Nelson's arm to get her attention.

"Is this the first time your daughter has been in trouble with the law?"

"Yes. I don't know what to do."

"That's all right; I will help guide you through this. How has she been at home?"

"Difficult."

"How so?"

"She doesn't come home when she's supposed to. Everything's a fight. She used to be an honor roll student, now she doesn't bother doing her homework. She says she doesn't have any and when I went to the parent conferences, her teacher said she hasn't been turning in anything."

"Does she use drugs or alcohol that you know of?"

"No, I've never smelled alcohol or pot on her. But I just feel like I don't know her anymore."

"Well, since this is her first offense, the Judge will be pretty easy on her. If you can't afford it, an attorney will be appointed to represent your daughter. But there are things we can help you with. There's a program for "Kids at Risk." Where we can work with the parents and monitor her more closely. Here is some of the paperwork, read through it and let me know what you think. I have attached my card."

"Thank you."

***

The court hearing went fast.

On their way home, Rebecca's mother asked, "Whatever provoked

4

you to shoplift, Becca? Now you will have a record and it will follow you around for the rest of your life."

"Oh, chill, Mom, you don't know what you're talking about. A girl in juvi told me that it was my first time so they wouldn't do anything to me. So I don't know what you're so upset about."

"Really? You were arrested Becca. Do you understand that?"

"Duh, of course I understand that, I spent the night in jail. What'ya think, I'm stupid? Besides, I don't want to talk about it anymore."

"But I want to talk about it."

"Well, talk away, but I don't have to listen. Just leave me the hell alone."

As the car pulled in front of their home, Rebecca jumped out slamming the door.

"Becca, don't slam the door, you're going to break a window. What's with you?"

She glared in the car window at me. "I told you I don't want to talk about it. Don't you have to go to work now?"

"Yes, I'm going, but we will talk about it when I get home."

"You might, but I'm not."

***

Two weeks later

Keilan promised to attend Mass with his mother and take her somewhere special for her birthday.

She smelled the coffee he made as she wandered sleepy-eyed into the kitchen, where he surprised her with a flat screen television decorated with a large red bow.

"My goodness Keilan, what are you doing up so early this

5

morning?" His mother said to him.

"It's your special day Mother, and I wanted to surprise you. I have the day all planned."

"Okay, tell me." She said clapping her hands.

"No, I want it to be a surprise."

He took her to Mass, then breakfast. The next surprise was shopping at Macy's where he bought her the purse she had been admiring. He slipped four crisp hundred dollar bills inside with a note. "Bingo money for St. Andrews."

Then they went to the park to feed the ducks and enjoy the sunshine. It was a full day, so he took her home for a nap, but told her he would be back later to take her to dinner.

She balked at him going to all the expense, but he said, "You can't deny me the right to spoil my favorite person in the whole world." and gave her a kiss on the cheek.

He surprised her with reservations at the Space Needle Restaurant. Where she could order anything she wanted.

They just finished dinner when his phone rang.

"Mother, I need to take this. It's work." He said as he got up from the table and headed to the observation deck to speak on the phone.

"Hello, Becca, is something wrong?"

"Yes, I'm worried about tomorrow."

"Come on Becca, I told you, just do exactly like we planned."

"I know but I'm just afraid that something will happen and my mother will find out. You know how protective she is. I have no privacy. She checks my phone daily. She's smothering me. I'm almost fifteen and mature for my age. You even said so."

"Slow down baby, it's going to be okay. If you do everything I told you, it will happen. You need to trust me, okay? The tickets are waiting at the airport. You and Connie will get on the plane in the morning, like we planned and you will be here five hours later. Your mom won't know you're gone until you don't come home, from Connie's. Then it will be too late. Are you still good with that?"

"Yes, but I'm still scared something will go wrong."

"Nothing will go wrong and we will be married right away and she won't be able to do anything about it. I know she will approve when she sees how much I love and cherish you. I've got to get back to my business meeting. I'll see you tomorrow afternoon, okay?"

"Yes, Keilan, I love you."

"Love you too, baby. Bye."

He headed back to the table to finish the evening with his mother. "I'm sorry Mother, what were we talking about?"

"We were talking about you giving me some grandchildren." She said with a sly look.

He gave a small chuckle. "You are a sneaky one." He said giving her a kiss on the cheek. "I'm working on it Mother, give me time." He said helping her on with her coat and heading out to the car.

"It was a wonderful day, Keilan. I am so blessed to have you for a son."

ANN KIDWELL

Chapter Two
Skye

I was excited to see Grammie, and the Seattle Airport. My sister and I watched the runway as Papa pulled into park. I pointed at the planes landing and tried to guess which one she would be on. While watching one of the circling planes, a speck the size of my pinky finger in the afternoon sky, I was able to see inside one of the plane's windows, which shouldn't have been possible. I could see the blemishes on a young girl's face and her long, chestnut brown curls. Her large, round brown eyes were crinkled in laughter. She looked about fifteen-years-old. I gasped, startled with the clarity of what I saw. My eyes pinpointed on *that* window in *that* plane, blinking, my vision returned to normal. This had been happening more frequently since my sixteenth birthday. *Spells*, I called them, when my vision is extra-ordinary.

Luna shook my shoulder. "Skye, what's wrong?"

"Nothing." I shook my head to clear my vision. "I was just daydreaming." Papa had parked the car in the short-term lot, and Luna was so excited she could hardly contain herself.

We walked towards the terminal and Luna asked, "Can we run ahead Papa?"

"No. I'm not comfortable with the two of you running loose in the airport, it's too easy to get turned around. Stay with me."

We checked the flight number for Grammie's plane, and we realized it was running 45 minutes late. We didn't mind, we were having a blast watching the planes take off and land. A large plane arriving from Detroit pulled up to the concourse; I recognized it by the plane's number located beneath the window as the plane I saw into. Watching as the passengers walked out, I saw the girl come through the open concourse door. She was with a blonde girl, who also looked about fifteen. Both carried backpacks and giggled at something on a cell phone. For a brief second, the dark-haired girl made eye contact with me. Then she turned with her friend, and made their way to the girls' bathroom.

I was curious who the girl was, and why I'd been able to see her through the plane window, I quickly told Papa I was going to the bathroom. The two girls were combing their hair and putting on makeup, and they didn't see me come in. I went into one of the stalls and listened. One girl said, "I can't believe we made it this far, where are you supposed to meet him?"

"He said to meet him at the Starbucks at three. That's an hour from now. How much money do you have left?"

I flushed and came out of the stall, walking up to the sink to wash my hands. The dark-haired girl's backpack had the name Becca on it. I stalled as long as I could, but just couldn't think of what to say.

The blonde girl reached into her tight jeans and struggled to pull out some cash and counted. "I only have thirty- five dollars and some change. What about you?"

"Yeah, that's about all I have left, too. He better show up or we're in trouble," Becca, the dark-haired girl, said as she bit at her bottom lip.

"Oh, he'll show because he loves you." The blonde one said. They both giggled as they applied mascara.

I didn't know how to approach them, so I left the bathroom, plugged my headphones in to listen to music, when Luna started jumping up and down and pointing to the plane that had just landed. "She's here, Grammie is here!" she squealed.

Watching the plane land and taxi toward our concourse, the loud roar of the two-engine prop plane drowned out my music, so I unplugged and got ready to greet her. I'm always excited when she visits, but don't show it like Luna does; bouncing around like a ping-pong ball with excitement. She's such a spaz sometimes.

The landing crew made quick work of getting the passengers and their luggage off the plane, and before we knew it, Grammie encircled us in a big hug. I just love her smell. She wears a soft floral perfume, and smells of the spearmint gum she chews when she's nervous. It was a unique smell that I only associated with her. She was dressed in slacks, a matching top and tennis shoes—she doesn't like fancy shoes. I found that odd, because mom said all girls love shoes. She's pretty cool for a grandmother, though. Not much riles her and she always makes people feel comfortable. I could probably tell her anything, and she wouldn't judge me.

"I brought something special for each of you," Grammie said, noticing one grandchild was missing. "Where's John?"

"We couldn't all fit in the car, so he's at his friend's house," Luna said, giggling.

Luna kept talking over me about what she planned to do for her visit. She tucked her arm through Grammie's and told her that she wanted her to come to her soccer game. I stuck by her other side and carried her walk-on luggage.

Papa gave his mother a hug, then pinned us with a stern look. "Give her some breathing room girls. We have to go pick up her luggage." Then he took her carry-on bag from me.

Luna pulled at her purse strap. "Grammie, will you play Barbies with me? You can have the blonde one."

"Of course I will," she said as she squeezed her in another little hug. She told me once that we made her feel young. She got around good for a 60-year-old. She has long, silver-blonde hair and loved to go hiking. I remember she once said it helps her stay physically fit so she can enjoy her senior years, and her rambunctious grandkids. That memory always made me smile.

Walking through the concourse toward the luggage claim, we passed a Starbucks. I saw the two girls sitting with a man at least 20 years of age.

Becca, the dark-haired girl, made eye contact and held it for just a moment longer than was comfortable for me.

I looked away as Grammie took me by the arm and steered us toward the baggage claim carousels. "Look for a black bag with a purple piece of yarn tied to the handle," she said. "It can put your excess energy to good use." She chuckled, shooting Papa a smile.

Grammie still worked a full-time job and cared for our Grandpa, so her visits are always short. She tries to squeeze a lot of happiness into each visit.

She was staying for five days, and then she'd return home to the east side of Washington State. She says Seattle is so green and beautiful with tepid weather, but where she comes from, it is cooler and drier. She loves living in Walla Walla, but it's lonesome without her sons and grandchildren.

Luna was the first to spot the bag, and rushed to beat me to it. Tugging it off the carrousel and dragging it over, Papa stepped in and clicked the wheels on the luggage so Luna could pull it. "That makes it a lot easier, doesn't it?"

With a giggle, Luna said, "Yeah." We made it out to the parking lot and loaded the luggage in the back of the Kia. With a little bit of space to spare, we headed home.

"Ryan, can we stop at *Walmart*? I need to pick up some groceries. The kids and I will fix dinner tonight. How does that sound?" Grammie prodded, knowing the way to Papa's heart was through his stomach. He loves her cooking; so when she comes to visit, diets and healthy eating are put in the closet until she leaves. "You can wait in the car, if you wish. The girls and I will try not to fill up the trunk," she teased.

The ride from the airport was filled with chatter about Luna's soccer games, and what our plans for this evening would be. I loved Grammie so much, and hated living so far from her. Even after mom and papa divorced, she stayed a constant stabilizing force for me. Their divorce provided shared custody of us kids, and for the moment, it worked. She is called the "Candy Grandma" by our mom, because her name is Candice and mom still loves and welcomes her.

Luna and I chatted about what to make, who was going to get to use the mixer, and who was going to get to lick the bowls.

Stopping at *Walmart*, it didn't take long to find everything that was on her grocery list, and we went through the checkout line in record time. On the way out, my eyes were drawn to the missing person poster the *Walmart* associate was pinning to the board. I stopped mid-sentence and grabbed Grammie's arm and pulled her to the board and pointed to a flyer being posted. "I just saw this girl! In the airport!" The poster was of Rebecca Nelson, and it read: "Missing from Detroit." Reading further, it described her as fourteen and thought to be heading to Seattle. She was a possible runaway and had been corresponding with an unknown male. She was accompanied by a friend named Connie Young. Her picture was also being posted.

"Grammie, I saw both of them. They were with a man in the *Starbucks* and in... in... the bathroom."

She squeezed my hand "Slow down, Skye, I can't follow what you're saying."

"At the airport, Grammie, I saw these girls get off the plane and go into the bathroom, and one was called Becca. Well, that name was on her backpack. They were talking and said they were meeting a guy that was in love with Becca. Then when we were leaving, I saw them sitting in the Starbucks with a guy. What should I do?"

Grammie turned to the lady posting the flyers and asked her about them. "They just came across in an email. We try to post them as soon as they come in," she said. Grammie asked the lady if she would make her a copy, pointing to the two missing girls' photos, so she could take them with her.

We headed to the car with copies in hand and Grammie filled Papa in on what I saw.

Papa said "We can stop at the police station; it's on the way home."

Papa parked in front of the Lynnwood Police Department, just a short distance from the *Walmart*. We all got out of the car and headed inside.

"I don't know if I can do this Grammie. You know I'm not good talking with strangers." I said. Although I've done professional ballet performances since I was about nine years old. That's performing, not speaking, and dancing is second nature to me. I felt extremely shy and introverted around strangers. So speaking to the police was going to be a challenge.

She grabbed my hand and squeezed it. "I'll be beside you all the time, so just tell the officer what you know, and don't be scared. You didn't do anything wrong."

"I'll try," I said.

The officer manning the counter looked up from the paper he was reading. "What can I do for you?" he asked Papa.

"My daughter saw these two girls at the airport about an hour ago," Papa said, laying the fliers on the counter. "We were at *Walmart* and they were posting these. So we came here."

The desk officer looked at the flyers and read the notice. "Hold on and I'll see if a detective can help you." He dialed an extension and spoke into the phone. "We have a young lady that believes she saw a couple of missing juveniles at the airport." He listened for a moment, then got off the phone and told us to have a seat and someone would be with us shortly.

"Grammie, will you stay with me?" I asked. Feeling panicked.

"Of course I will," she said.

About five minutes later, a petite attractive lady in her thirties came out and led us back to a conference room. She was slender and had short, bobbed, straight, blonde hair and wore a badge on her belt. "I'm Detective Alexandra Prosser, with the Missing Persons Division." Nodding to me and Luna, she said, "But you can call me Alex."

Alex asked us if we would like a soda and if she could get coffee or water for Papa and Grammie.

Luna asked, "Do you have orange pop?"

"I'll check to see, if I don't have orange, do you like *Mountain Dew?*" asked Alex, with a smile on her face.

"Oh yeah," Luna said, clapping with excitement. Alex came back with two sodas for us.

Luna asked, "Are you a real cop?"

Alex smiled at Luna. "Yes, I am, but detectives don't wear uniforms," she appeared to anticipate Luna's next question.

"Now, let's get down to business," Alex said. "Which one of you saw the girls on the flyer?" she asked looking at me and Luna.

"I did," I said, lifting my index finger from the table and looking down at the flyers.

"What's your name?" Alex asked with a smile.

"Skye."

"What a beautiful name. Who picked it out?" Alex probably sensed my shyness and wanted to put me at ease. "What nationality is it?"

"Umm, I don't know. My Papa is part Cherokee and my mother is Japanese, but I think my Grammie picked it out," I said in a quiet whisper, tapping her on the shoulder.

"I'm part Chekapee, too," Luna said, which always garnered a laugh from me.

"Okay, Skye, this will be recorded." Alex said. "It's just a formality and it helps me in my note taking. Is that okay with you?"

"Okay." Looking around, I didn't see a camera. "Where's the camera?" I asked, beginning to relax.

"Oh, there's a little camera where that red flashing dot is." She said, pointing to the corner of the room. "It's all automated and it is downloaded on a computer drive somewhere. Will it bother you to be recorded?"

"No, I guess it's alright."

"Is Skye the only one that saw the girls?" Alex asked.

"Yes," said Papa. "The rest of us weren't paying attention, except watching for my mother's plane."

Alex nodded. "Maybe I should just speak with Skye then."

"Can my Grammie stay with me, please?"

"Sure she can, and if your Dad wants, he and your sister can wait in the lobby."

Papa nodded and stood. Taking Luna's hand in his, he told Alex, "We have groceries in the car. Maybe Luna and I should take them home and come back. How long do you think it will be?"

"It will probably take an hour," said Alex.

15

"All right, that's what we'll do then." Papa got up to go and shook Alex's hand.

Chapter Three
Alex

Skye squeezed her grandmother's hand and looked anxious. I could hear her stomach gurgling. She looked nervous so I need to start simple.

"What's your full name and age?"

"Skye Ayala Frost. Almost 18."

"Okay Skye, tell me what you saw today?"

"We were waiting on my grandmother's plane—it was running late. At the gate next to us, people were getting off a plane. It said over the loud speaker it had arrived from Detroit. Two girls were getting off the plane and they looked familiar."

"What do you mean familiar?"

"Well, um, not familiar... It was... they caught my eye. I don't know, maybe because they looked so young and all."

"Okay, go on."

"They went into the girls' bathroom, so I followed and I heard them talking. The dark-haired girl had a backpack with the name Becca on it, so I thought it was her name, but I didn't know for sure until I saw the flyer at *Walmart*."

"Do you remember anything they said in the bathroom? What did they talk about?"

"They talked about meeting a guy who was in love with Becca. They also talked about only having thirty-five-dollars. Oh, and Becca said she was supposed to meet him at Starbucks at three o'clock."

"That's good Skye. Then what happened?"

"I left the bathroom because I couldn't think of any way to

introduce myself. Then, Luna and I were watching the planes land and take off."

"How much later did your grandmother's plane land?"

"About a half-hour."

"So tell me again what caught your attention about these two girls." I needed to push for a reason she noticed them in the first place, but she seems guarded. What is it she isn't telling me? She didn't answer right away and sat fidgeting with her soda can. Then she looked up at me. "Skye, did you understand the question?"

"Um, yes, I'm not sure. I think I liked the girl's long, curly, dark hair. I've always wanted curly hair. I don't know what got my attention."

I'll move on. "Is that the last you saw of them?"

"No, after Grammie's plane came in, we headed to the baggage carousel, and when we passed by Starbucks, I saw them sitting at a table with a guy."

"You saw them sitting with a guy?"

"Yeah."

"That's good. Can you describe the guy they were sitting with?"

"Well, he was thin and sort of... looked like a young Johnny Dep. He was handsome and had olive skin. I'm not good with ages, but he was maybe twenty-one. He had a tattoo of a ribbon with the name Rebecca in it and a web tattoo on his wrist. He was about my papa's size, um… 5'10" and had straight, dark, brownish hair, a little over his ear. He looked like he could be Spanish or Italian with a thin nose, full lips." I could feel myself blush at the details I gave her.

"That was a really good description. You have a lot of details."

"Um, thank you. I've been learning to draw profiles, so details are everything."

"Do you think you would recognize him if you saw a picture of him?"

"Yes, I think I would."

"Okay Skye, with the computer age and automation, I'm going to have my partner upload some photos that match the description you gave me. It will take about ten minutes, would you like another soda?"

"No, I'm fine. But I do need to use the bathroom."

"Alright, I'll take you down the hall."

Nick, my partner had been watching the interview and was in the process of uploading the photos. *If she can identify him, it may give us the lead we need to rescue the girls. She saw the guy! That's a bonus I didn't expect.*

While waiting on Skye to return to the interview room, I struck up a conversation with her grandmother. "Candice, where did you fly in from?"

"Walla Walla."

"Oh, I love Walla Walla, it's beautiful there and all the wonderful wineries. I believe it's better than Napa Valley. It's closer at least," I said. "Have you lived there long?"

"Oh about 30 years, and I think that makes me a native, right? It's hard to become a native in a small community." She says, smiling.

"I think I would agree with that." She seems personable and had a warm smile.

Skye came back into the room and appeared more relaxed. "Your grandmother was telling me she lives in Walla Walla. It's different than Seattle, isn't it? A little drier?"

"Yeah, and she has horses. I love to visit her, it's in the country."

"I bet you do. Do you ride horses?"

"No, but I would like to someday."

The intercom buzzed and Nick said the photos were uploaded. "Hang on Skye, and I'll get signed into the file." After a little fumbling the file opened. "Are you ready to look at some photos? Nick put together... it looks like about 50 photos that match the description you provided." I turned the screen so she could easily go through the photos. "Just press the forward arrow to view the next one. Take your time, I don't know if he is in there or not, so don't feel that you have to pick one."

"Wow, that was fast! I expected to look through the big books you see on television."

I had to laugh, "Yeah, we are starting to come into the Twenty-First Century. If you have any questions just ask."

It took about 20 minutes for her to go through all the photos that had been uploaded. In the meantime, I was making notes on things to follow-up on. Candice seemed relaxed and took out a book she had in her purse.

"I'm sorry, he isn't any of these." Skye apologized.

"Skye, do you think you could describe him to a sketch artist with enough detail to get a likeness?"

"I think so."

"Well, the artist is in another city and wouldn't be available until tomorrow morning. Do you think you could come back in?"

She looked at her grandmother for direction.

"We can do that. What time?" Candice asked.

"Nine o'clock tomorrow morning. Is that too early?"

"No, we'll be here."

Candice shakes my hand and I escort them to the door. Handing Skye my card; "If you remember anything, just give me a call, alright? The littlest detail can sometimes give us the lead we need. I'll see you in the morning."

***

After the Frosts left, I had several good leads from Skye that my partner and I could follow. In the meantime, I briefed patrol about the case and provided them with copies of the missing girls' flyers.

Skye was holding something back, but I couldn't get her to tell me. I would have to follow-up on that.

I contacted the Detroit Police Department handling the report on the missing girls and they said the girls' cell phones had not operated since right after they arrived at the airport, therefore, no longer traceable. Although there was a frequently called number from Becca's phone to a phone that had been purchased at a *Staples* store in Edmonds, about three miles from here, which was also no longer traceable. The store had a record of that purchase, but said the buyer paid cash and the clerk was checking with the manager to see if they had a video for that day. He will call me back as soon as he hears from the manager.

The airport video also needed to be reviewed. Skye's observation of the two girls sitting in the Starbucks would narrow it down.

There was urgency to follow-up on every lead before the trail got too cold. So this would be a long night. This appeared to be more than a runaway child case. I know how fast they can disappear underground into the abyss of Seattle's human trafficking. This was the break we've needed to find these bastards, the trail is still fresh enough to get leads. Skye's descriptions were detailed, and if we can get a photo or artist's drawing of the suspect, we may find the girls before it's too late.

Nick, my partner, had called and updated the FBI; ICE (Immigration and Customs Enforcement); and DHS (Department of Homeland Security), which take the lead in many human trafficking cases as they cross state and international borders. They shared details they had, and were following-up in the Detroit area. My task force had the lead on this one at the moment. Working together with other agencies and sharing information was the key in resolving some of these cases.

***

I walked into the conference room where my task force waited. I grabbed the fresh coffee someone had placed in front of my chair, probably Jodi, and gave her a nod and a smile.

"We have a lead in the case of two runaways that may be at risk for trafficking. This is a classic case, fifteen-year-old Rebecca Nelson was groomed online and in social media, to leave her home in Detroit and fly to Seattle along with her friend Connie Young. The girls' means of communication had already been severed and they may already be impossible to find. The pimps have gotten smarter and are selling their victims online to a select clientele. We got to work smarter or we'll lose two more children to these monsters."

Pointing to Detective Loney, "You check the websites that traffickers use: *Backpage, Craig's List, Snapchat,* and *Kik.* I already assigned a detective to the Staples store and one to the airport to check security tapes."

It had become so much harder to find these victims since the pimps were marketing these girls on the dark web. At least when they were on the street, the officer patrolling the area had a chance of seeing them. If we can find them, they can be spared the horrors in store for them. Thank God, Skye saw those missing girls' pamphlets.

The Task Force had recently joined an undercover sting operation with the FBI, HSI and ICE, dubbed *Operation Web Weavers.* At the center of the investigation was an individual known as Weaver. He has operatives running a human trafficking network of underage minors in all 50 states. This network is suspected of kidnapping children across the US, using an elaborate scheme of social media contacts to lure young girls and boys. I think this is who has Becca and Connie. The key evidence was the tattoo of a web on the man's wrist that Skye saw and the way Becca was groomed and lured, matches Weaver's MO.

As I reflect on all my training and seminars, there is enough work chasing leads that we could use twice the manpower. The hope is to eventually get a handle on these ever-evolving predators. But as soon as we have the electronic sites they operate on monitored, they change to a different site. And now the gangs might be involved. This isn't restricted to men either, many female perpetrators are also involved in this horrendous trade.

***

Having worked my way up the ranks, starting as a dispatcher for the 911 Center, I've been in the trenches. I passed the officer's exam then went to the police academy. Then I worked patrol for five years and passed the detective's exam. That is where I'm needed. My specialty was in missing persons and I worked hard compiling a task force to handle the Human Trafficking aspect, which has been going on for decades but was just beginning to receive the attention it needed in the Seattle area.

"Alex." Nick snapped his fingers in front of my face. "You seem lost in thought."

"Yeah... We have the potential to save these girls because one witness was paying attention." I said.

"That witness, and you. You are tenacious, where does that passion come from?"

Nick's question took me back to my first missing girls' case. I never liked to talk about it.

Pausing to get my focus on the past, I said, "It was my first case and it was awful. We had been called out to a home where three young girls were held in the basement. They were shackled to an old furnace. Emaciated and left to die. From their condition, they had been there for days without food or water. A man walking his dog had heard a tapping on a pipe coming from the house. The house was abandoned and boarded up and in an area of high drug trafficking. The man looked through a dirty basement window and saw movement. He contacted the police and when they arrived, expecting to find transients or meth addicts, they found an eleven-year-old and two twelve–year-old girls starving and lying in their own waste." I took a breath, before I could continue my story.

"We arrived as the girls were being loaded in the ambulances and rushed to the hospital. One of the twelve-year-olds didn't make it. She died from her injuries after being beaten and starved. The girls had been taken from a labor camp where their parents had reported them missing. Afraid of deportation, the parents had been reluctant to report their missing children. But when the girls weren't back after two days, they called the police. The parents thought that Coyote, an alias for Jose Pineda, had taken them because they hadn't paid his fee for smuggling them into the US."

Reaching for a tissue, I tried to get through the story. "When I think about those girls, I get sick. They had been repeatedly raped and beaten. I'd held the hand of the dying girl. She cried saying 'I'm sorry. Tell my mama and papa, I tried to be strong.' They were never able to catch the men that did this, and this case continues to haunt me. That's what fuels my passion to help put an end to this atrocity." I tried to explain, tears filling my eyes.

Nick placed a consoling hand on my shoulder.

"Just last week, I gave a training and informational course on *Human Trafficking in the U.S.* to the Task Force and a Citizen's Awareness group. Do you remember the citizen's group astonishment that this was happening in their own backyard?"

Nick nods. "I do, but it was an intense training and I think the citizen's group was having a hard time absorbing the information that this was happening in the US, much less their city. It painted an ugly picture they didn't want to really know about."

I felt weary but needed Nick to understand why this is so important to me. "To me, this is my mission. I need to save as many as I can, and bring awareness to the communities. It's been a slow process getting people to accept the fact, but remembering the child that died in my arms keeps me motivated to get the word out."

Chapter Four
Skye

We were home before 6:00 p.m. so I had time to call my friends and tell them about the runaway girls and going to the police department.

Then I turned the lights off and lay thinking about the two girls on the plane. *Why would they run away from home? And why was I obsessing over who Becca was? I couldn't explain to the detective why she had my attention.*

How could I see her at such a great distance? Am I going crazy? This has happened a couple of times when I was walking at the mall. I would get these pictures in my mind of someone I don't know and it would only last for a few seconds, and the vision background was usually outside the mall, but in front of a store I wasn't near. There is no sound from the person I am seeing, except a soft drumming hardly perceptible with the traffic noise. Then there are the dreams that are so life-like they scare me. There is always a soft drumming in the background, but not like any music I've heard before. These dreams always have a person I don't know or recognize in them. The person appears to be sad and I feel their sadness, but I don't know why. I can't hear anything they are saying, but they are usually sitting in a corner hugging their knees. Most times they are teenage girls. I have seen one boy, he wasn't crying, but seemed angry and pounding his fists into the floor, he looked about 15-years-old. I have some really good friends, but no one to talk to about this.

With Mama and Papa divorced, I don't want to bother them, they already have too much to worry about. Divorce sucks. If I can just get through my senior year and graduate, I can help them, instead of being a burden. Maybe going into the Navy would be a good choice. They have a linguistics program I could try. I already speak Japanese fluently. Plus, the Navy would pay for my college. Or with luck, I'll get the scholarship to pursue dancing.

Dancing is what's gotten me through this past year. Now I'm dealing with bouts of depression and Mama has to pay for a counselor.

Ugh, I need to turn all this worry off. Grammie says worry steals your joy from what is happening now...

Grammie! We have a special connection and she'll understand. With that decision made, I drifted off but the smell of tacos woke me up.

Semi-refreshed, I joined the family in the kitchen. Luna had helped Grammie make a taco salad and set the table, chatting the whole time about her new friend, how John wouldn't do his chores, and playing soccer. Blah blah blah.

Accustomed to quiet, I was surprised Grammie wasn't overwhelmed with the chatter, but she seemed to keep up with her.

The taco salad was yummy. She had put cut-up apples in it. We love her cooking and get tired of Papa's. We gorged ourselves on dinner which seemed to make her happy. After dinner and dishes, Grammie and I moved into the kitchen to make Southern Style Banana Pudding for tomorrow's dinner. Papa's favorite. We talked about the missing girls and where they had gone, and about why they would run away.

"I really liked detective Alex and hoped I would get the description of the man right, but I couldn't tell her the real reason why the girls got my attention." I said.

Grammie stopped what she was doing and turned to me. "The real reason, what do you mean?"

"It's probably nothing and no one would believe me anyway."

"Oh, honey, I would believe you. What is it?" She put her arm around me and looked me in the eye.

"It's only happened a few times and I'm not so sure I wasn't imaging it." I paused trying to figure out how to explain it. "When the plane was in the sky, before it landed, I could see the girl, Becca, in the window."

"What do you mean you could see Becca?"

"Well, when we first got to the airport, Luna and I were watching the planes take off and land. Becca's plane was about the size of my pinky and you could barely tell it had windows, but for some reason, my vision focused on her window. I could see her clearly and even the small mole below her eye. It was like looking through a telephoto lens or maybe a telescope. I could see her talking to someone. It was just weird." *Now Grammie is going to think I'm nuts.*

She wrapped her arms around me again and gave me a big hug. "I believe you, sweetie. Sometimes things like that happen. Maybe your mind was telling you to pay attention to this girl. You know our minds are powerful tools. Let's finish this pudding before we burn it. Did you tell your dad?"

"No, I was afraid he wouldn't believe me."

"That's alright. I believe you, and we'll talk more in the morning when we've had some rest. How about that?"

After we set the dessert in the refrigerator, Luna and I played with each other's hair. Papa had fallen asleep on the sofa, so Grammie went to take a shower. We planned to have popcorn, watch a movie, and then go to bed.

Luna knocked on Grammie's bedroom door. "Are you ready to come watch a movie? Skye made popcorn with butter."

"All right Luna, I'm coming."

She came out of her room dressed in a nightshirt and robe. She smelled like fruity shampoo and lotion. Her hair was wet and tousled and she found the comfortable loveseat to sit on.

Luna snuggled up to her. "Can I comb your hair while we watch the movie?" Luna asked.

"You sure can. What movie are we watching?"

"A yukky romance, of course. Skye has a boyfriend and his name is Preston…something." Luna said, shrugging her shoulders.

Without thinking, I stuck my tongue out at Luna as she was sticking her finger down her throat making vomiting noises. She is such a baby sometimes. I curled up in the corner of the sofa where Papa was laying almost asleep.

Luna combed Grammie's hair for a little bit, then moved around to sit in her lap, where she fell asleep. Soon my eyelids felt heavy.

"Skye wake up, it's late. You need to go to bed so we can be at the police station promptly." Grammie told Papa to take Luna and put her in the bed as she doesn't wake easily. Then I heard her tell Papa they needed to talk.

***

Candice

"Ryan, would you like a cup of tea?"

27

"No, I'm good Mom. I'll turn off the television and savor the quiet for a moment."

"Ryan, we've got to talk about Skye. It's time."

"Time for what?"

"It's time to tell Skye about her heritage. She's exhibiting her gift." I watched Ryan absorb my last statement. "Have you told her anything? Is she prepared in any way?"

"No Mom, I thought we had more time. I wasn't sure she would have a gift…I never did. Why, what happened? How do you know?"

"You know the girl she saw in the airport? She saw her—close up before the plane landed. It wouldn't be physically possible without her manifesting her Cherokee gift. I believe it is the gift of sight."

Chapter Five
Candice

I was really enjoying my trip to Lynnwood and my grandkids, but Skye's confession about *seeing* the girl, revealed the gift that she was manifesting. This changed everything to do with my trip. When a Cherokee's gift focuses on an individual, it is a sign that the person's life is in peril. In order for Skye to use her gift, she needs to understand and be able to focus that gift.

Before going to bed, I called Aaron, my eldest grandchild, to see if anything unusual had happened to him. He said, no, though I noted a hesitation before he answered. Past observations of my grandchildren had served me well. Aaron was hiding something. I invited him to Cherokee, North Carolina with me and Skye.

He was between jobs at the moment and thought it would be fun to see where I was raised, so he'd agreed.

"I'll text you the information within the next hour. Ryan is making the reservations now. It will be good to spend some time with you too, and an added bonus will be getting to see the Great Smoky Mountains."

I hung up with Aaron and looked over Ryan's shoulder while he booked the reservations online.

"Ryan make the reservations for three, Aaron is going with us too."

"Mom , are you sure you're up to this kind of trip? You haven't been back there in years."

"I'll be fine and it will only be for four days. Get us as close to Cherokee, North Carolina as you can and I will rent a car and drive the rest of the way. It will be good for the kids to see their Great Grandmother, she hasn't seen Skye since she was an infant and she has never seen Aaron."

"Okay, Mom the closest I can get you is Ashville, on such short notice, will that do?"

"That'll do."

There really wasn't time to notify my mother, Takena, I would be coming, but I knew in my heart that my mother would be expecting us.

Takena is the Wise Woman of the Wolf Clan and she has an uncanny ability to know what the future would bring. Where she lives on the reservation, she doesn't have a phone and I usually correspond with her by letter. Though, in an emergency, I can have the tribal police get in touch with her.

Ryan got all the reservations made. Tomorrow he would take us to the airport right after we finish at the police department.

***

Skye

I woke thinking about Becca and Connie. I'd dreamed they were looking out a window in a house. They looked happy, especially Becca. I grabbed some paper and a pen from my school bag and tried to write down all the details from the dream while they were still fresh. I'm not sure what good it'll do, because it was just a dream, but Grammie said the mind is very powerful. Besides, what would it hurt to have it, just in case.

It's only six o'clock in the morning... Ugh, why did that dream have to wake me up? Is that bacon I smell? Yummy. I love it when Grammie visits.

Grabbing some sweats and running a brush through my hair, I took off to find where that wonderful smell was coming from. *Wow, Papa's up.* Papa never gets up early. The smell of bacon must have woken him up, too. Grammie was busy turning the bacon in the pan. Smartly dressed in a matching pantsuit and her hair was lying in soft curls around her shoulder. How does she do that?

"Wow, look at this feast! How long have you been up? Don't you ever sleep? We don't have any roosters out here to wake you." I said. We're always joking about living in the country.

"A kiss for the bacon-cooker please," She said, pointing to her cheek.

I gave her a kiss and hug, and reached for a plate.

"Now, Skye, sweetie, I need you to pack some clothes. We are flying east to visit your great-grandmother, Takena, right after we go to the police department. Aaron will be going also," Grammie said, giving me a good morning hug.

"Wow, really? You mean to North Carolina? Mama said we went

there when I was a baby, but I don't remember it. Why are we going there?" I asked, getting excited.

She smiled. "I think it's time you learned about your Cherokee roots, and there is no better place than on the reservation."

"Is it just us three? What about Luna and John?"

"John's still at his friend's house, and they had planned to go camping, and Luna is going to stay and keep me company," Papa said. "Speaking of Luna, wake her up so she can get dressed, too. She is going to stay with the neighbor because we all can't fit in the Kia. Grab some breakfast while it's hot. I'll pick up Aaron while you guys are at the police station. Then it's a quick trip to the airport. Vamoose, as Grammie would say."

ANN KIDWELL

Chapter Six
Becca

Connie and I stood in front of Starbucks waiting for Keilan to show. I stood on tiptoes to try and spot him. I finally saw him and let out a squeal. His smile made my stomach flip. I bounced on my toes and held onto Connie's arm. I could talk to him online and on the phone, but in person he was way too cute for me. He was so hot. Connie actually squeaked next to me and said, "Oh my god…he came."

I'd been really nervous about meeting Keilan. We'd Skype, but actually seeing him in person was better. He looked a little older in person than I expected, but he had the most beautiful brown eyes, and they sparkled when he looked at me. Unlike the skinny boys at school, he was muscular like a football player. I bet he worked out a lot. He wore a crucifix around his neck with a matching earring in his left ear. He had on a short-sleeved shirt which showed his muscles. Rebecca was tattooed on his right forearm. *My name was tattooed on his arm.* I can't believe that he's in love with me.

Keilan walked up with a shy look and asked, "Are you my gift from Detroit? Becca, sweetie, you are so pretty." I didn't know what to say, he just took my breath away. "Remember what I told you on the phone, we can't draw attention to ourselves. But I so want to hug you right now." He turned his attention to Connie and said, "Thank you for taking care of my Becca. Would you two like some coffee and something to eat? I know you spent more than five hours on the plane?" We each gave him our order and he told us to have a seat in the back corner, as he was concerned about being caught on camera. "I don't want them to come and take you away from me, now that we're finally together. I'll be right back." He said and headed to get our order. I was so nervous, I didn't know if I would be able to swallow.

"How do I look, Connie? He is soo gorgeous. Did you see my name tattooed on his arm? Oh, I feel like I'm going to be sick."

"Chill Becca, you can't puke on him. Get it together. Yes, you look good except for that broccoli in your teeth." Connie said, smiling, trying to get me to relax. "You'll be fine and he probably just wrote your name on his arm with a black sharpie." She said, laughing.

"Cut it out, Connie." I said, slapping her in the arm. "No joking, do I look alright?"

"You look more than alright, you look beautiful," Keilan says, coming back with the coffee and setting it in front of us, giving me a wink. I felt I would melt right there.

He sat next to me and I could feel his eyes on me. I felt self-conscious, so I was looking out at the concourse and we were discussing the rain and the difference in temperature from Detroit, when I saw the young, slim girl with long, black hair that had stared at me when Connie and I got off the plane and in the bathroom. She appeared to be with her family. She glanced at me as she walked past, with a questioning look in her eyes. It puzzled me for a few seconds until Keilan placed his hand on mine and his eyes followed my gaze to her. The girl turned her head away when the older lady got her attention.

Keilan asked, "Becca, who's that girl?"

"I don't know, I just saw her when I was getting off the plane."

Keilan said. "How would you both like to go to the mall? We will stop by my sister's house as she lives close to a large mall and she'll take you to buy some new clothes. I'm sure your backpack doesn't have your whole wardrobe in it." He laughed.

We were so excited that Connie and I both looked at each other. "You don't have to do that," I said, feeling like we couldn't have him spending more money on us. He'd already bought the airline tickets, and now he wants to take us shopping. "You've already spent so much on us, how can you afford that?"

"No worries, I've been saving for the day when I could spend money on my special girl. Besides, my job pays well, and I can afford it." Keilan squeezed my hand under the table. His hand was so warm and I could feel my face blushing. He just made my stomach feel like I swallowed butterflies. No one has ever made me feel this way.

Under Keilan's directions, he left first and we were to follow behind, but not too far. We walked out of the airport. Keilan told us where the hotel shuttle would be parked. We were to get on and they would drop us off at the hotel and he would pick us up there. He said he didn't want to park where there were cameras. So we followed him to where the shuttle was waiting. He walked past and we got on board. He gave us an umbrella so the Seattle rain wouldn't spoil our hair and he said it would shield us from the cameras too.

We were scared but followed his directions to the letter. We went into the hotel then out a side door where he was waiting. Keilan opened the door to a brand new dark green GMC Denali and we jumped in. It still had that new car smell, like leather. I was trembling with excitement as I grabbed Connie's hand.

"Oh, you should probably give me your cell phones. They can be traced by the GPS." Keilan put his hand out to us.

"But I have all my contacts and pictures in there," I said, reluctant to lose all my friends' addresses and phone numbers.

"You don't need mine do you, Keilan?" Connie asked.

"Yes, I do. You don't want them to trace your phone and find Becca, do you? I can turn it off and remove the batteries, and then when things are safe, I'll give them back. Okay? Besides I have new *iPhones* for you, I was going to give them to you later today. Now you've spoiled the surprise," he said, making a sad face.

"Go on Connie, give him your phone. We can transfer our contacts to the new *iPhones* when we get them," I said as I handed him my phone.

Keilan removed the batteries and put them in his pocket. "Now, let's go shopping so you can get all the things young ladies need and many pretty things they don't." He put his arm around me and gave me a squeeze. I am the luckiest girl in the world. "Getting out of the airport worked like a charm, just like I said it would," Keilan said, kissing my forehead.

He was very affectionate toward me in the truck, brushing the hair away from my eyes and gently caressing me in a shy hug. He told me I was even more beautiful than he imagined, and my face got flushed. He said he couldn't be affectionate in the airport because we might raise suspicion. Connie was sitting in the back seat and I felt a little uncomfortable in front of her.

"Connie, you can buy some pretty things too. I have some really nice friends that have been waiting to meet a beautiful blond to settle down with. What kind of guys do you like? A blond surfer dude or a dark-haired mystery man? A pretty girl like you, can take your pick."

"I don't know what I like. As long as he's not fat, and he likes Mexican food, we will get along." Connie said with a giggle.

We went by his sister's house and she was waiting. We dropped our backpacks off and got in her car and headed to the mall. Keilan said he had some errands to run, but Mandy would take care of everything. "Mandy, get both the girls some clothes and shoes. I know how much you girls love your shoes," he said, laughing. He gave me a peck on the cheek and a quick squeeze. "Buy something sexy in white for our wedding night with some high heels. You're so pretty and you're all mine. I want to make all the guys jealous. So buy some short skirts and short-shorts to show off your beautiful legs. My God, you are gorgeous." I was embarrassed when he said this and looked at Mandy to see what her reaction was.

"C'mon Keilan, I got this. You're embarrassing the poor girls," Mandy said, giving his shoulder a shove.

Shopping with Mandy was like going shopping with Santa Clause. She told me whatever I wanted she would buy for me, plus clothes and shoes for Connie.

We shopped and bought all kinds of clothes and a pair of four inch stilettos that Mandy said Keilan would love. I don't know how I will ever learn to walk in them though. When I looked in the mirror, I looked much older than fourteen. I hardly recognized the girl looking back. My mother would kill me if she saw me in some of those clothes. "With those clothes on, girl, you will turn heads," Mandy said. She picked out most of the clothes for me and Connie. "What the hell, Keilan gave me the credit card and told me to spend, so that is what we are doing," she said.

The trunk of Mandy's car was loaded with bags and boxes. We must have spent hours at the mall.

"Now that the shopping is done, we're going to head back to the house where you girls can get some rest. Keilan had a few errands to run to set up things for tomorrow. It is going to be a big day, we'll be seeing some sights and he has a surprise planned. He wanted to do things the right way. That way no one would be able to separate you two."

We drove for about fifteen minutes and arrived back at Mandy's, which was a small ranch style house with a dirt driveway hidden among some trees. It was down a winding road and the houses were farther apart than they were in Detroit. The area was beautiful, but woodsy, like being in the country. The furniture was sparse and there weren't any pictures hanging on the walls. It had three bedrooms and two baths, so Connie and I would have to share a room for now. Keilan said this was Mandy's house. His was much larger and on the coast.

Mandy said, "Get some rest. Keilan's bringing pizza home for dinner."

We were so excited, we couldn't wait to try on our new clothes and shoes and model them for each other. I was in a dreamy state and having a hard time believing my dream was coming true. "I knew I loved Keilan, but had no idea he was so rich. He had a new truck and we are going to get married in a fairy tale wedding. Oh, I wonder where we will live." I didn't expect an answer, I was just thinking out loud.

Resting was out of the question. The five-hour flight and our arrival made the adrenaline course through both of us. Connie was a little sad because she wasn't meeting anyone, but Keilan said that he knew a lot of guys, and they were anxious to meet a pretty blond girl from the East.

The next hour we spent trying on clothes and shoes and giggling and talking about everything. How the flight went, and how good it was to finally be in Seattle. We compared Detroit to Seattle and how much better the air in Seattle smelled. We also talked about how the rainy weather made my hair curly. We both agreed that Seattle looked nothing like the places we had been back east.

We finished just as Keilan showed up with pizza and soda. We ate and played video games and watched some TV. It was getting late, so Connie said, "I think I'll go to bed and let you two be alone." Then she went back to the room we shared. Mandy said she had a date and left right after Keilan returned with the pizza.

Keilan wrapped his arms around me and pulled me close. "Becca, baby, you are my world. I can't believe that you're finally here with me." He gave me a passionate kiss, and it felt like my world was spinning.

I could hardly speak so it came out in a whisper, "I know, I can't believe it either."

"It seemed like a lifetime since I found you online, but that's in the past, here we are with our whole life before us." Then he gave me another long kiss. "Tomorrow, I have a surprise for you. You are a princess and deserve to be treated like one."

He cleared his throat and pulled away. "Oh, God, I want you so much now. I don't know if I have the will-power to wait," he said, getting up abruptly from the sofa.

"I know, Keilan. I want you too, but we can wait a little bit longer, can't we? Am I being a prude? All the girls at school have already slept with their boyfriends. I just wanted it to be special, you know?"

He sat back down and touched my face softly and said, "No, I know you're right. I want to be your first, but at the right time. How are you still a virgin? You're so beautiful, and I would think the guys would be fighting over you." He said, as he gave me a long, slow kiss. He drew back and laughed, "Are you blushing?"

"Yes, you're embarrassing me. It may be old-fashioned, but I wanted to save myself for marriage."

"That's not old-fashioned, that's admirable. I admire your convictions. What about Connie, does she share your convictions? I don't mean to pry so if you don't want to answer, I understand."

"I get embarrassed talking about sex, or making love. I'm not sure she shares my convictions because she had a steady boyfriend for about six months and she told me he was the only one she'd been with… sexually."

After that Keilan got quiet. Did I say something wrong? I wasn't sure what just happened, so to break the uncomfortable silence, I asked "Can I get another soda?"

"Sure, bring me one, too," he said.

As I got up from the sofa, I heard a click down the hall toward the bedroom, but I didn't see anyone. Keilan looked back there too.

"Never mind on the soda, Becca, I think we better go to bed so we can get an early start tomorrow."

"Oh, okay, I am starting to get sleepy anyways," I said.

He got up and gave me a big hug and a long, slow kiss. Oh, how he takes my breath away. "Sleep tight Princess, and I'll see you in the morning," he said as he kissed me with little pecks on the forehead, nose, and mouth. "And sweet dreams."

Chapter Seven
Alex

Skye and her grandmother arrived promptly at nine o'clock. She still appeared shy and introverted, but the sketch artist quickly put her at ease. They shared a mutual interest in drawing. Skye gave a good description of the man she saw with the girls. When they'd finished, Skye affirmed his likeness. "Here, make copies of this sketch and distribute it to the shift sergeants and put an all-points-bulletin out on him within a hundred mile radius," I said to my assistant.

I walked Mrs. Frost and Skye to the door and thanked them for their help. "If you think of any other details, Skye, feel free to give me a call. Have you still got my card?"

"No, I gave it to Grammie."

"Well here's one for you. If something comes to you, you can reach me anytime on the cell number. Thanks again. Your observations and details have been a big help." She tucked the card in her pocket and gave me a shy smile.

We had spent last evening at the airport where we obtained video footage from the airport and *Starbucks* which we showed Skye and she had pinpointed the guy for us, but the images were grainy and he seemed to know where the cameras were and had kept his back to the camera. Checking the cameras outside of the airport hadn't been much help either; he'd been shaded by an umbrella. Those videos, stills, and sketches had been given to the FBI to run facial recognition.

Just after the Frost's left, the *Staples* store called and the video footage was available for us to review, so I headed over there. The phone had been paid for in cash. When it started playing, the clerk said he remembered the lady. He said he hadn't seen the woman in the store before. "She was skinny, seemed nervous and with sores on her face. Ya know, like she was "tweaking," like a meth user."

We'd been given a copy of the video and our forensic officer had produced stills of the woman, which was also distributed to patrol in the area near *Staples*.

A plethora of leads gained in the last eighteen hours, and none of them had panned out. We had lost the trail on Becca and Connie. My gut told me we were close and this guy was too good and too careful. He'd done it before, I was sure of it.

We had gotten the cell phone records for Becca's phone, but that had been a dead end too. We'd gotten a ping on a location in the area around the airport and had found the destroyed phones, where they had been crushed in the street. No prints. The girls had disappeared like a puff of smoke.

Just when I had given up hope, a vice officer recognized the woman that had purchased the phone from *Staples*. She was an addict and he brought her in for questioning.

I walked into the interview room with a cup of coffee and a notepad. "Hi Lisa, my name's Alex and I would like to ask you a few questions about a phone you purchased about three months ago at *Staples*. I know that was a long time ago, but you may be able to help us in our investigation. Here's a drawing of the man we are looking for. Was he the man that you purchased the phone for?"

"I don't know, man it was a long time ago." She squinted at the drawing and was scratched her arm. "It might be him."

"Take your time, Lisa. I'm going to show you a video of a person in the *Staples* store that looks a lot like you. Maybe that will refresh your memory."

"Okay, then can I go? I could be in trouble for talking to the cops."

"Sure this should take only a few minutes." I cued up the video and she got up close to the computer.

"Yeah, that's me. I remember now. This white dude came up to me and said he would give me fifty bucks and some smack to buy him a phone. He wrote the name of the phone he wanted and told me how many minutes he wanted. Then he gave me cash and dropped me off in front of the store. He had a big roll of bills. I showed the man behind the counter the note and he got me the phone. Can I go now?"

"Okay, in a minute. Did the man look like the guy in the drawing? Do you remember what he was driving?"

"Yeah, that's him. I remember now. He was good-looking and seemed in a hurry. He had a big truck. It looked shiny and new."

"What color was the truck?"

"It was dark. Maybe green, I don't remember, can I go now?"

"You don't know the make of the truck?"

"No, I told ya, I don't know nothin' more."

"Thank you, Lisa. Nick will you show her out?"

The phone hadn't been on since right after the girls met him at the airport.

ANN KIDWELL

Chapter Eight
Connie

Feeling like an outsider in Becca and Keilan's world was putting it nicely. I love Becca, and we have been friends since first grade, but Becca can't see anything or anyone but Keilan. Running away had been her idea. She wanted to be with Keilan so bad that she was willing to risk everything. Becca had a good family that loved her, and a mother that only wanted to keep her safe, but she felt they just didn't understand her. I adore Becca's mother and many times wished I had a mother like that.

My family is dysfunctional to say the least. My mom and dad are divorced, and mom stays out most nights and my sister and I are pretty much left to raise ourselves. I don't get any mothering from my older sister either. She spends all her time with her boyfriend. I can't stand her boyfriend because I've seen him shoot up drugs and I'm afraid that he will get her using too. I have just been feeling more alone lately, which is why I let Becca talk me into running away.

Now I'm on the other side of the country and I don't know if running away was my answer. I took an immediate dislike to Mandy, Keilan's sister, she just seemed angry all of the time. Something just doesn't feel right. Growing up on the streets of Detroit made me a little more streetwise than Becca. I shouldn't have agreed to do this, then, maybe Becca wouldn't have gone without me. I just want to protect her.

I'm tired from the trip and the time change. I left Becca and Keilan alone in the living room and thought I would get some sleep. Only, I can't turn my head off. I'm too wound up from the excitement of the day, and a little homesick, missing my own room. I laid down again and tried to sleep, but needed to go to the bathroom now. I feel funny about disturbing Becca, because the bathroom is across the hall and I'm afraid they will hear me. Shit, I gotta pee, so I'll just have to disturb them. Cracking the door slowly to try and sneak down the hall, I heard Keilan ask Becca if I had been with anyone. *If I had been intimate with anyone.* This question sent a stab of fear through me that I can't explain. Why would he ask a question like that? I tiptoed across the hall to the restroom, and prayed he wouldn't hear me.

I just made it in time. Looking around the restroom, it didn't have any decorations or anything personal. I guess it had toilet paper, so that's something. Everyone goes through medicine cabinets, don't they? At least that's what mom said. So, I peeked. There wasn't anything in there either, some old Band-Aids and dental floss. Who lives in a house and doesn't put anything in the medicine cabinet? This is just weird.

Then I heard him telling Becca something about getting some sleep, so I peeked out and his back was to me and I closed the door with a quiet "click."

***

Becca

I shook Connie awake about six the next morning. "Connie wake up, it smells so good outside. I opened the window, smelled the fresh rain and hear the birds chirping. It's nothing like Detroit. Come and smell."

Stepping to the window, Connie took a deep breath of the morning mist. As we looked out the window I saw a large, white bird sitting on a low branch of a fir tree. The bird stood out white against the green background.

"What kind of an owl is that? I've never seen anything like that?"

"I don't see an owl, where is it?" Connie asks.

"Just over there on the second branch near the trunk of the tree, you can't miss it. It's white with large green eyes."

"I still can't see it."

"Oh wow, it just flew away and its wings were huge. I can't believe you couldn't see it, it was huge. I never heard of a white owl!"

"Becca, I don't know what time I finally fell asleep last night, but I was tired and remembered feeling homesick. I know my mom isn't the greatest, but I still miss her. I don't want to ruin things for you, but I'm not sure this was such a good idea," she whispered.

"Oh, come on, you'll get over the homesickness. How about we try on some of the clothes we didn't try on last night, it will make everything better." We tried on the new clothes, deciding what we should wear. It seemed to have taken Connie's mind off going home. At least I hope it did. Seattle weather in July, I hope these shorts are okay.

About an hour later, Mandy tapped on the door, "Would either of you like some breakfast? I made coffee, toast, and eggs."

We came out and smelled the food cooking and the hot coffee. Becca asked, "Can I take a shower before breakfast?"

"Sure, use the main bath and Connie can take one after you. Keilan left earlier as he was working on a surprise for you."

I headed to the shower.

**

Connie

"How is the weather in Seattle in July? Can we wear shorts or does it get cold and rainy? I asked Mandy.

"It's not supposed to rain, but you never know about Seattle. How do you like Seattle so far?"

"It's a lot different than Detroit. The streets are cleaner and there isn't litter all over the place, like Detroit."

"What is it like living in Detroit? I've heard there's a lot of crime."

"Sometimes. You just have to stay out of certain areas where there are drugs and higher crime. Actually, I live on the edge of a suburb, so it isn't real bad there. I don't like the weather there. The summers are short and hot, and the winters are really cold."

Mandy asked, "So you don't do drugs?"

"I've smoked a little weed, but nothing more than that."

Mandy continued asking questions, she seemed to be warming up to us. I wasn't sure she was happy about us coming. "Did you have a boyfriend that you left behind? A pretty blond like you must have been popular at school."

"Not anymore, I had a steady for about six months, but he cheated on me."

"Connie, did you see my earrings?" Becca said coming into the kitchen. Her hair and makeup looked great.

"No, you left them on the dresser. She loses everything," I said to Mandy. Then turning back to Becca, "That's why she should keep them in her ears."

"You know, you sound like my mother," she scoffed.

"Wow, Becca, don't you look beautiful. I love the way your hair lays in curls down your back. Is that natural curl or do you get it permed?" Mandy asked, touching the curls that reach to the small of Becca's back. "Are you hungry? There is still some bacon and eggs left."

"No, it's natural, but sometimes I wish it was straight. Yes please, to the bacon, eggs and some coffee if there's any left?"

"Sure. Are you excited about being here with Keilan? He has been talking about you non-stop since he met you online. He said you were beautiful, but he has a knack for exaggeration. But he wasn't exaggerating about you."

"Thank you," Becca said.

"Are you nervous?" Mandy nodded to the plate of food Becca was pushing around with the fork.

"Maybe a little. I want everything to work out. It just seems like things are going so fast. You know?"

"Sure, I understand, but that's Keilan's way. When he sees something he likes, he has to have it right now." Mandy said. "He should be back in about an hour."

I got up from the table and said it was my turn and headed toward the bathroom to get dressed.

Chapter Nine
Connie

"Oh, I can't wait to see what the surprise is. Maybe he has a house on the beach. He doesn't worry about money, because he gave his credit card to Mandy and she spent a ton of money on us." Becca said, looking dreamy eyed. "I am so in love with him and he loves me. He asked if I've ever seen the Pacific Ocean, so I think he may be planning to take me to the ocean. He told me to bring a sweater so I won't get cold. He is always so thoughtful. Just think, by tomorrow I could be married." She let out a squeal as she dances around the room.

I reached over and grabbed her arm. "Chill. You haven't heard a single thing I've said, have you, Becca? I'm still worried. We don't know anyone here, and we really don't even know where we are. Doesn't that bother you? We rely only on Keilan to provide for us. What if he dumped you tomorrow, then what would we do? If I just had my phone, or any phone, I could call my mom and at least let her know I'm alright."

Becca stopped and said, "I'm sorry. It'll be all right, you'll see. You could probably call from a burner phone, when we get one, so our moms won't be able to trace it," Becca said. "Keilan must have forgotten to give us the replacements. What kind of surprise do you think he has planned?" Damn, that girl can't think about anything but Keilan. I wish I hadn't let her talk me into this.

There was a tap on the door, and then it pushed open. "Keilan just called and said he would be here in about five minutes. Are you ready, Becca?" Mandy asked.

"It'll be just a minute." Becca giggled as she squeezed my hand. "See, it'll be okay."

"Be sure and pack all your stuff as you won't be coming back here," Mandy said through the door.

When Keilan arrived, Becca and I had our stuff ready in backpacks and a couple of day bags, Mandy had given us. We loaded it into the back seat of the truck, which left just enough room for me. Becca got in the middle of the front seat with Mandy next to the door.

"Becca, baby, I have a big surprise for you and Connie. Today will be unforgettable." Keilan squeezed and kissed Becca's hand and looked at me through the rearview mirror.

Becca was beaming with happiness, but Mandy's disposition had changed from relaxed and friendly to sullen and quiet and she kept her eyes on the floor in front of her. I was happy for Becca, but something didn't feel right and I couldn't put my finger on it.

Keilan drove through winding roads with trees everywhere. Not like a forest, because there were subdivisions and stores, and I was amazed at the green of Seattle. About fifteen minutes later, Keilan pulled onto a highway with lots of traffic.

"Keilan, did you forget our cell phones?" I asked.

"I haven't forgotten. You'll be getting them later this afternoon. Then you can transfer all your contacts to them," he said, again, making eye contact with me through the rearview mirror.

We drove on the highway for about fifteen minutes more and then I noticed we were passing glass sky scrapers and lots of traffic. The towns were cleaner and more modern than Detroit. The air smelled fresh with a slight dampness to it, but not hot and humid. "Is this still Seattle?" I asked Keilan.

"No, this is a suburb of Seattle. All these cities run together in this stretch of highway. I'll let you know when we get to where we're going, so settle back and enjoy the ride, it'll be awhile. You can't ruin my surprise, okay?"

"Okay." It didn't feel like he was asking, but politely telling me to shut up.

We drove for about an hour and I needed a bathroom break. "Mandy, is there a rest area; I need to go to the bathroom?"

"Hey Keilan, stop at the next rest area. We all need a bathroom break."

Becca and Keilan were chatting away, and he was teasing her about getting married. He often glanced up at the mirror, watching me as he drove. His looks weren't friendly and his stare made me uncomfortable. As if to say, *You're not going to screw this up for me.* It made the hair on the back of my neck stand up.

I wanted to be alone with Becca so we could talk, but we were rarely alone. I felt like an outsider in this situation. Maybe at the rest area we would get a chance to talk. I started paying attention to where we were and the highway signs. South Interstate 5 going toward Portland. I didn't like not having a phone. Something wasn't right, I could feel it.

We pulled into a rest area that was busy with large trucks and cars. It's Friday, so I figured it was filled with people going out for the weekend.

Becca and I headed into the restroom; Mandy said she needed a smoke so she would wait outside. I quickly told Becca, "Something isn't right."

Becca was in front of the mirror, smiling like a fool. Her eyes never left the reflection. "What do you mean?"

"We have no phones, and Keilan doesn't like me, I can feel it."

"Aw, you're just imagining it. I just think he wants to be alone with me is all," Becca put her arms around me.

"No Becca, I can feel it, we need to get away from him and Mandy. Something is WRONG." I grabbed Becca's hand. "We could sneak away and ask someone to use their phone and call my Mom. She'll know what to do."

Becca got mad and started to cry. "Why are you DOING this? I can't leave Keilan, I love him and he loves me. You'll RUIN everything. What about my wedding?"

"You don't understand Becca, I can feel it. It's just this… whole thing doesn't feel right. I don't know exactly why, but I can't stay here. Come with me. Let's sneak out and ask a trucker to use their phone."

"No," Becca said. "Keilan would never do anything to hurt me." Becca began to shake and tears glistened in her eyes as she stared at me. "I don't want to get married without you at my wedding. You're my best friend. Please, stay, you'll see. You're wrong about Keilan."

"How do you know Becca? You don't really know him at all. I am your best friend, which is why you need to trust me."

"I do know him. He paid for our airline tickets and spent all that money on us at the mall, and he wants to marry me. He loves me."

The bathroom door opened and Mandy yelled, "Hey what's taking so long in there? Keilan's ready to get back on the road."

"Be right out!" Becca yelled back.

"I can't, Becca. Come with me."

"No way."

I grabbed her arm and I began to cry, "Please, Becca."

"No, I won't leave Keilan."

"Alright, will you distract them so I can get away?" I said. "Tell them I started my period, and you need to get my backpack. Then get Mandy away from the door."

"No, I can't. You have no idea where we are, or what to do. Where will you…"

She looked into my eyes. "Alright, go then. You've already ruined my day. You're just mad because you don't have someone that wants to marry you. I'll get her away from the door, and you can go to hell for all I care."

Mandy yelled again. "Becca, come on. Is something wrong?"

Becca wiped her eyes and checked in the mirror, set her jaw and glared at me, then walked out of the restroom. "Connie started her period, and she gets nausea and really bad cramps. She needs her backpack to get her clean undies."

I peeked out the door and Mandy headed over to the truck where she unlocked the door, and Becca rifled through her backpack as if she is looking for supplies.

I ducked out of the restroom and hid behind a shrub. I could see the truck and Becca as she headed back toward the restroom with my backpack.

I stayed in the shadows thinking I would make my way to a semi-truck and ask the driver if I can use his phone or take a ride with him out of the area. I don't know why, but I felt my life was in danger. I saw a semi pull in and decided that was the one I would try. Just as I left the cover of the shrubs, a girl with a short skirt, knee-high stiletto boots, and a cropped top approached the truck. I was about five feet from them and could hear her asking if he would like a little company. She looked like the hookers I'd seen on Jefferson Avenue in Detroit.

Maybe a truck driver might not be my best choice, so I slipped back into the shrubs just as I heard Becca calling my name.

"Connie where are you, where'd you go?"

I saw a small pickup with a camper shell on it. An older couple got out and walked their dog. Not sure if I could make it without being seen, I took a chance and ran to the back of their truck and duck behind it.

"Please, please be unlocked," I whispered to myself as I reached for the handle of the camper shell.

The guy who owned the pickup turned and headed in my direction asking his wife, "Want soda or water?" She replied yes to water. I backed up to a small hedge about six feet away, just as he reached the back of the pickup. He flipped the window up and reached into the cooler and removed a bottle of water and a soda then shut the window and headed back toward his wife.

Maybe I should just call out to him or his wife and ask for help or to use their phone. What am I going to say? "I just have this feeling that things aren't right?" Or maybe I could ask them to use their phone because I'm a runaway and want to call my Mom. That might work, but who knows how Mom is going to react. She's told me numerous times, you get in a mess, you get yourself out. Don't come crying to me to get you out, blah blah blah. If I can just get to a town maybe get a hold of the police they will get me home, or a runaway hotline, I think I heard of that on TV. Ugh, right now I just need to find a safe place to hide where Keilan can't find me. Eck he makes my skin crawl.

I removed my shoes and sprinted from the hedge to the truck, then quietly lifted the window and slid inside. I don't think anyone saw me. I could still hear Becca calling my name and Keilan's shouts sounded angry. I moved away from the window and crawled to a corner and burrowed beneath a canvas cloth between some paint cans.

Damn, I should have got the license plate number of Keilan's truck. I peeked out the window, but the truck was at the wrong angle and I couldn't see the plate.

The *Scatter Creek Rest Stop* was the name I saw on the sign when we turned in here. I made sure to remember the name so I could tell the cops where I was. It is pretty busy. I hope there is enough activity they won't find me. I heard the couple come back and get in the truck. When it started up, I breathed a sigh of relief. Just as I let out my breath, I heard a slap on the side of the truck.

The lady rolled down her window. "I'm sorry to bother you, but did you happen to see a blond girl with white shorts around here?" Becca asked. "She was just here and now she's gone."

"No, I'm sorry," said the woman. "I didn't see anyone. How old is she? Is she a little girl?"

"No," Becca said. "She's 17."

"No, I'm sorry. We were just walking our dog, but we'll keep an eye out."

Becca thanked them, then headed back toward Keilan.

The little truck pulled onto the highway and I released the breath I was holding.

I shook and cried until I fell asleep under the painting tarps, listening to the tires on the highway. I awoke when the truck stopped. There was talking and I heard gas being pumped into the truck. I peeked out of the small sliding window in the camper shell. Without my phone, I had no idea what time it was, but the sun was setting and the air was getting cooler and damper. There was a highway sign that said Exit 82.

I ducked back under the tarps thinking they might get something out of the cooler and I didn't want to be discovered. While pumping gas, the man told his wife they could get dinner at the restaurant across the street. She agreed and said, "It's cool enough to leave Crackers in the truck in the shade, and we can bring him a doggy bag. "You'd love a treat, wouldn't you Crackers?" She said to the little dog. The fact that I had run away two days ago was really starting to sink in. I began to shake and I wasn't sure if it was the cool air or that I was scared.

Did I make the right decision? How could I leave Becca there, what if he hurts her? I'm scared and wished I was home and Becca had come with me.

I felt the truck pull into the restaurant lot. The couple got out and after speaking to the dog, promising to bring him a doggy bag, they went inside the restaurant.

I did not know where I was. I decided to take a chance by going into the restaurant. I needed to use the bathroom before I wet my pants. *Oh, God I wish I was home. I just needed things to be normal again."* Every instinct in *my body had told me to get as far away from Keilan as I could. He was nice, maybe too nice. It just didn't feel right. No one is that perfect.*

I'll run into the restaurant, find a bathroom, then a phone. I waited a few minutes and climbed out of the truck and walked inside the restaurant, following a family, trying not to draw attention to myself. I saw the bathroom sign and was grateful it was so close to the door, since I had no shoes on. I had left them at the rest area.

Thank goodness, the bathroom was empty. I went into a stall and began to cry and couldn't stop. I put a hand over my mouth to stifle the sobs.

What can I do now, thousands of miles from home? No money, no phone, please, God help me.

Wiping the tears from my eyes and blowing my nose, I noticed a flyer posted on the stall door *Polaris Project, National Human Trafficking Resource Center Hotline. If you are being held against your will and/or you need help call us at 1-888-373-7888 or text us Be Free 233733.* Little tear-off strips with the phone number dangled. I had no phone, no purse, no ID. Keilan took all that, and said it was so they couldn't find us.

"Oh God, I want to go home." I cried into my hands again. Then I heard the door open.

I quickly flushed, blew my nose, and wiped my face. While I washed my hands and face at the sink, the lady from the truck came to the sink beside me. There was no way to hide my swollen red eyes. The lady looked at my reflection in the mirror. She gasped.

"Are you okay?" she asked. "What's wrong? Are your parents out there?" She pointed out the door. "I can get your mother."

"No, she's not here, my mom's in Detroit," I said, trying to keep my voice from shaking.

"Are you okay? Did someone hurt you? Do you have someone I can call for you?"

The questions struck a hollow pit in my stomach. The tears wouldn't stop flowing. The lady wrapped her arms around me and made comforting coos.

"Everything will be all right, now. You're going to be okay."

I felt exhausted.

"My name is Brenda, what's yours?" the lady asked.

"Co… Connie." The tears began to slow.

The lady, Brenda, looked to be about fifty or sixty years old. Her brown hair, a short shoulder-length cut and her eyes were kind. At this moment, I felt safe.

Brenda pointed to a strip of paper in my hand that I hadn't realized I had pulled off in the stall with the phone number on it. "What's that? Do you need to call someone?"

I looked down at that strip of paper.

Brenda asked, "Do you have a cell phone?"

I shook my head. "Not anymore, he took it."

Brenda pulled her cell phone out of her pocket and handed it to me. "Here, you can use mine, while I go to the restroom."

I took the phone and dialed the number on the paper in my hand. I wanted to call my mom, but was afraid to. I was afraid mom would hang up on me.

A lady answered the phone, "*The Polaris Project,* can I help you?" I hesitated. I didn't know what to say. "Please don't hang up," she said, "we can help you."

I clutched the phone and said with a shaky voice, "My name is Connie, and I ran away from home."

"Are you in a safe place to talk."

"Yes."

The woman on the phone took my personal information and where I was from. "We show a report stating that two girls were spotted at SeaTac Airport. Did you fly to Seattle?" Just as Brenda came out of the stall the volunteer asked me, "Where are you calling from?"

I didn't know so I handed the phone to Brenda and said, "They want to know where we are?"

Brenda took the phone. "Yes, it's off I-5 in Centralia, Washington, exit 82."

Then Brenda handed the phone back to me. "I'm searching the missing children's database and I've found the flyer that went out on you and Rebecca Nelson? Is she with you?" The lady asked.

"No, I'm alone."

I could hear the lady typing. She said, "We are making contact with the lead detective on the investigation. Stay there and we will contact an officer to come pick you up, okay?"

"Okay," I said to the lady on the phone.

I handed Brenda back the phone and asked, "Can I stay with you? They're sending an officer out to get me."

"Sure you can. Have you eaten anything?"

"No, but I'm not very hungry."

ANN KIDWELL

Chapter Ten
Skye

After Grammie and I went to the police station and gave a description to the artist, Papa was waiting in the car with Aaron to drive us to the airport. We talked about how the artist that did the suspect drawing was so talented and then I filled Aaron in on what I saw yesterday at the airport and *Walmart*. It didn't take long to get to the airport as the traffic was light, and we grabbed a quick snack before boarding as this flight didn't serve lunch.

Grammie, Aaron, and I boarded the plane for North Carolina. Things happened so fast we didn't get a chance to discuss the trip. Grammie had told me there would be limited internet access in the part of the reservation we were going to at Cherokee, North Carolina, which meant that our phones may not work. Not sure if I'm gonna like that. I'm used to having my phone. She also said once we got in the air, she would tell us about her growing up on the reservation. It was a subject she never really talked about much in the past.

We settled into our seats. I got the window seat and Grammie sat between Aaron and me. The trip was non-stop and we would arrive in about five hours. That would put us on the reservation after 7:30 p.m. with the time difference.

"Skye, when you told me about seeing Becca, when she was still in the plane, that was when I made the last-minute decision to go to Cherokee, North Carolina. You were exhibiting your Cherokee gift."

"What is a Cherokee gift?" I asked. This conversation seemed to get Aaron's attention as he took out his earphones and started listening to our conversation.

"The Cherokee share their lineage through the telling of stories. Many generations ago, the Great Spirit saw to bless certain Cherokee people with special 'gifts' to help them to defeat their enemies and survive. Not all Cherokees are given a gift and many times it will skip generations as it did with your father. Your Great Grandmother, Takena, the Wise Woman of the tribe, possesses two gifts, which is very rare."

"What are her Cherokee gifts?" I asked.

"She has the power to see into the future, and can decipher dreams. She will know that we are coming and will be preparing for our visit."

"How do we know if we have a Cherokee gift?" Aaron asked, alert and interested.

"Not all Cherokees have a gift, but when they manifest one, it usually has to do with the six senses. They are enhanced powers that are above human powers." She continues. "As with Skye, she was able to see at a far distance and, therefore, her gift dealt with her sense of sight."

"I thought there were only five senses, Grammie?" I say.

"Yes, Skye, you're right with reference to what modern man has chosen to believe. But there is the sixth sense, which is called ESP or Extra Sensory Perception. Some believe in it, and others do not."

"What does ESP mean?"

"Umm, you perceive something that is not tangible or that you can't explain how you know, you just do. Like a feeling or a knowing about something, but you really have no basis to prove how you know this."

Aaron joins the conversation. "Is it like you know something is going to happen, but you don't know how you know this?"

"Exactly, but it can be expanded to include the spiritual world and a heightening of our other five senses."

"That's rad, Grammie. So you're saying the sixth sense or ESP is real?"

"I'm saying those that possess this sixth sense, say it's real. Don't disbelieve just because you can't touch, see, hear, taste, or feel it." She says as she pats Aaron's knee.

I notice a change in his demeanor and attention. He's really interested in this stuff.

Grammie points to Aaron's phone, "Can you do that Google thingy and look up sixth sense on your phone?"

"Yeah, I'm on it," he says.

"Grammie, what is Takena like?"

"Umm Takena, she is feisty and has a fire that burns from within. She's passionate about her people and the Cherokee ways. She's soft when she needs to be soft, and she's hard and won't back down when she gets a notion in her head. One of the strongest women I have ever known. Lord, how I have missed her."

"Why have you stayed away so long and not seen her?"

"Well, that's ancient history. I won't go into that too much now, but we had a falling-out when I married your Grandfather. You've never met him, I was married to him for only seven years and he gave me two fine sons. He was one of those things Takena wouldn't back down from. But that's a tale for another time." She said. "I need to rest my eyes for a few minutes now. We can talk more later, okay?" She said, letting out a weary sigh.

"Yes, get some rest," I say, kissing her on the cheek.

Grammie closed her eyes and Aaron plugged back into his phone. I sat staring out the window wondering what it would be like on an Indian Reservation. What having a Cherokee gift meant. So much had happened in the last 24 hours. When I close my eyes and fall asleep, there is always a low drumming in the background and my dreams seem so vivid. Maybe all my questions will be answered soon.

***

Aaron

While on the plane to North Carolina, I hoped that I would figure a way out of the quagmire I've gotten myself in. I'd promised myself that when I returned home, I would regroup and get a job and make something of myself. Getting away and seeing where my family came from may just be the incentive I needed to pick myself up and move forward. With the drone of the jet engines and the rock music from my headphones, I revisited the last couple of years.

Smoking weed had been a steady state for me this past year since my breakup with my high school sweetheart. Five years we'd been together, then boom; it was over. I hadn't seen that one coming, but I should have. During one of my sober periods, I remembered, she was always working after school and I was sitting home playing video games. I'd let her carry the full load. If it weren't for these damn voices! That's just an excuse, I know it is. Kelly told me as much. Her exact words, "Aaron, I can't do this by myself, I'm tired and all you want to do is sit around, smoke weed, and play video games. I don't make enough money to keep supporting us both. I've been harping on that for years, and now I'm through. Take care of yourself." Oh, how my world had crumbled when she'd left, and yet I'd done nothing to change my life except more of the same. I'd buried myself in a cloud of smoke to silence the voices.

I'd considered that I might be schizophrenic, because that's what hearing voices meant. I'd been afraid to tell Kelly or anyone else for that matter. When I was 17, I'd asked Grammie if there were any mental disorders in her family tree, kind of feeling her out. She'd said not that she knew of. Some depression, but that was it. When she asked why, I'd told her we were studying DNA anomalies at school.

I wasn't doing anything with my life, just sitting around waiting until my Dad kicked me out of the house. He kept hounding me to get a job. Maybe I had some of that depression she talked about. Going to North Carolina should be fun. I've never been east of the Mississippi.

When I was at my lowest, she sensed it, because she called and asked if I wanted to go to Cherokee, North Carolina with her and Skye. I needed to do something, so why not?

***

Skye

About an hour later, the *Fasten Your Seatbelt* sign comes on with an audible dinging and the pilot says they are climbing to forty thousand feet as they are encountering turbulent weather. The dinging wakes Grammie up with a start.

"It's okay Grammie, the plane is flying above a storm." I say.

"I'm sorry, I wasn't snoring was I?" She asked.

"No, you weren't snoring," I said with a giggle. She is so paranoid about sleeping in public because she snores.

"Will you tell me a little more about the reservation?" I say.

"I haven't been to the reservation in a long time. The last time was when you were only three months old and I was to give you your Cherokee name. Just a wee little one and so precious," Grammie gave me a squeeze and a kiss on the cheek. "I'm happy I get to go home and see my Mother, it has been more than forty years since I left for good."

"Why is it important that we go now, Grammie?"

"I feel it's time for you and Aaron to see where your father's family comes from. My side, of course, still, you need to know this part of your heritage. Also, Takena isn't getting any younger, and she wishes to see her Great Grandchildren. But most importantly, you are exhibiting your gift and Takena is the person that can answer all your questions and teach you about your gift."

"So she will teach me?"

"Yes. I'm sorry that I hadn't told you this earlier. But the urgency of going now is because your gift was focused on the young girl on the plane, and that indicates that she may be in some danger."

"Does Aaron have a gift also?" I looked over at Aaron. He had earphones in, so he wasn't following our conversation.

"I don't know if Aaron has a gift or not, I just felt he needed to learn about his heritage, too." She glanced Aaron's way. "He has always been at loose ends, and maybe meeting Takena will inspire him to learn the ways of the Cherokee and give him direction."

All this talk of a Cherokee gift is kind of scary. I really don't know anything about my Cherokee heritage though. But I wanted to know why I could see in that plane. Whew, at least I'm not going crazy!

I hadn't spent much time with Aaron lately, because we don't live near each other anymore. His Dad and Stepmom divorced and he doesn't come around as much. Grammie said she's worried about him because he seems depressed and moody since she saw him last, so she thought he could do with a change of scenery too.

After I'd told her about seeing Becca, she played it down and I wasn't sure if she believed me or not. She just gave me a hug and told me sometimes things happen that we can't readily explain. When I got up this morning, she had the trip to North Carolina booked and planned.

Last week, I'd spoken with Aaron on the phone and he'd confided in me that he was ashamed that he wasn't as successful after he graduated. He just hadn't found what he wanted to do, he'd said. But I feel he is holding something back, too. Maybe he'll tell me during this trip, or at least Grammie, what is bothering him.

When I'd questioned him further, he said he was reluctant to share with Grammie things that he thought were only in his head. I gently prodded him and told him that he could trust her, that she only wanted to help. He said he would think about it. She is always there for us. My cousins and I have talked about how we can tell her anything and she will not judge, but will offer advice or suggestions.

Aaron would celebrate his twenty- first birthday this October. He loved Grammie, but he really didn't spend much time with her, although he lived closer to her than the rest of us. So this is a treat for both of us to spend time with her.

We talked a little bit more about the Reservation and the beauty of the Smoky Mountains, then Grammie said she was going to catch-up on some of her reading. I don't know where she gets her energy.

Chapter Eleven
Skye

When we arrived, Aaron and I were in awe of the beauty of North Carolina. We were used to the green of Seattle and the forests of fir and pine, but this was a different kind of forest with a different feel. I felt an unfamiliar pull. Feelings akin to going home resonated deep within me. A peace settled over me that I was a part of something much bigger than myself. I know that sounds silly, but that's the only way I know how to put it.

We gathered our carry-on luggage and headed to the car rental. We were only staying three days, so we hadn't checked any luggage. We had navigation on our phones, so between mine and Aaron's phone, we didn't need a map. Grammie laughed as we directed her to the reservation. After that, we lost cell reception but she knew the way from there.

We pulled up to a simple but tidy home. An old Cherokee woman sat in a chair in the yard as if she'd been expecting us. Grammie put the car in park, jumped from the car, and ran up to hug this elderly woman. It had to be our Great Grandmother, Takena, that she'd spent the whole trip describing. She was in her 90s, and the Wise Woman of the Wolf Clan. I could tell that Grammie's heart ached from the time she had spent away from her mother.

Takena held out her arms in welcome to her daughter. They embraced and they both couldn't stop crying. Takena wore a full Cherokee skirt in bright vibrant oranges and reds which came to her ankles and a peasant-like blouse with multiple strands of beads around her neck. Her long, gray hair still had a few strands of black and was worn in two braids with leather laces wound around the bottom. The braids hung to her waist. Brown, wrinkled skin adorned her face and her deep-set shining eyes were alert. A toothless smile lit up her small fragile features.

Grammie introduced Aaron and me to our great-grandmother. She was so tiny and frail but had a spark in her clear, brown eyes. Her looks were deceiving because she was sharp and didn't miss anything. I got the feeling she knew what I was thinking. I have never met or known anyone in their nineties. She and her daughter hugged and cried while both were trying to talk at the same time. It gave me such a warm feeling.

I shyly stepped forward into Takena's embrace. I bent down to give her a hug and I was afraid she would break. She put me in the mind of a fine china doll only with tan brown skin and a leather wrinkled smile. She hugged me and said, "Oh my little one, you carry a lot of the Cherokee features and you are so stunningly beautiful and so unaware of your beauty. I saw you many years ago when you were an infant. It was at your first naming ceremony where your Grammie gave you the name of Skye. I have a keen insight into the human heart and yours is pure and kind. You honor me in seeking my guidance." She hugged me tightly and kissed me on the forehead.

Takena looked from me to Aaron and held out her arms. Aaron looked down and shuffled stiffly toward her and allowed himself to be hugged and patted, too. "My eldest great-grandchild, you are tall and strong and quiet. You are definitely a warrior. You remind me of a young warrior I fell in love with many years ago. Your great-grandfather, only your eyes are as blue as the sky." She had to reach up to hug him and stood on her tiptoes, and I saw a stray tear go unchecked down Aaron's cheek. "I see within you many questions and I hope that you will get answers to those questions during your visit. Your coming was not unexpected. My dreams foretold that I would receive three visitors and they would be from our clan, and that you would be among them. I hope that you find the peace you seek here," she said, pulling away, and looking at us.

"I am so happy to finally meet you both. Come, let's go inside in front of the fan. This summer heat and humidity will be hard on y'all." Takena guided us inside. "I made some iced tea anticipating your arrival. It's sweet, so I hope you like it." Her voice was clear, and yet, had a very soothing ring to it. Though, it surprised me because she sounded much younger with a deep southern twang.

"You kids are spoiled with your air conditioners so this will take some getting used to," Grammie said.

We hadn't eaten so Takena took out plates and served up some traditional Cherokee food. "These are referred to as the Three Sisters: corn, beans, and squash. They have sustained our tribe for hundreds of years. Of course we spice them up a little more with wild onions and spices." Takena proudly gave us our plates.

As we sat around eating, I could hear some soft drumming in the back ground. "Should I call you Great Grandmother or Takena?" I asked.

"You may call me Takena, as that is what all the children around here call me," she said, giving me a radiant toothless smile. "Great

Grandmother is a mouthful."

With the heat and the long trip, we were tired and Takena suggested we take a short nap. She said it would refresh us. She made a pallet on the floor for Aaron and me, and Takena and Grammie napped in the bedroom. It didn't take long before we all fell asleep to the music of the forest and the drums.

As I drifted into a quiet sleep, I dreamed that I was looking down on the beautiful green of Seattle. The best way I can describe the green is it looks like the green of an emerald. I am high above looking down and I can see a few house roofs, but my eyes are drawn to a large highway. It looked like Interstate 5 that I have traveled many times. The green gets closer and I'm looking at a rest area which has some large semi trucks and many cars. As the ground gets closer, I'm surprised to see Becca and Connie. Becca and another dark-haired female walk up to a dark, green truck. My attention is drawn to Connie leaving the restroom and hiding in the bushes. Then I see the sign *Scatter Creek Safe Rest Area*. The dream follows Becca to a green truck with the license plate I can see clearly.

"Skye, Skye, wake up sweetheart, you were moaning loudly. Were you having a bad dream?"

I told Grammie about my dream and asked, "Do you know what any of that means? Is it from my gift?"

"I don't know if it was just a dream or your gift, but it may be important. I am going to go call the detective, so write down everything you can remember about the dream. Can you tell where this rest area is?"

"Um, I think it is on I-5. There was a sign that said *Scatter Creek Safe Rest Area*, it didn't look familiar, but the highway did. Also, on the green truck it had GMC Denali on the emblem and I could see the license plate number." I was telling Grammie all that I had seen in the dream. About the girls and the one named Connie getting in the back of a different pickup, as I was writing it all down.

"Well, Skye, I'm not sure how I am going to get the detective to believe me, but I think it is important enough to try. It may help to find those girls."

***

<u>Candice</u>

Takena just came out of the bedroom as I was going out the door.

"Mother, I have to step out and get some cell phone reception, so do you know where I need to go?"

"Head up the hill where you used to play in the stream. That cove should be high enough to get some reception," Takena said, pointing toward the hill behind her house.

I gave her a hug and a kiss on the cheek. "I need to run an errand and will be back shortly." I grabbed a piece of fry bread and headed out the backdoor. The forest was the same as I remembered it, and I knew the hill I needed to climb to get cell service. I pulled Detective Prosser's card from my pocket and dialed the Lynnwood Police Station.

"This is Detective Prosser, how may I help you?"

"Hello detective, this is Candice Frost. Do you remember me?"

"Yes, of course. How can I help you?"

I hesitated for a few seconds, but decided to go on, as it may mean something. "Um, yes, I'm not sure how to put this, but you might want to check for the young girls at a rest area along Interstate 5. At *Scatter Creek Safe Rest Area* and look for a dark, green GMC Denali truck with the following license plate number. I can't explain how I know this just yet, but it may be a clue."

"What, how do you know this? Where did you get this information from? Can you come to the office and bring Skye?"

"I'm sorry I cannot, I'm calling from North Carolina and won't be back for another couple of days. Cell service is hard to find here, but I will call when I get back to Washington," I promised. "I just thought it might mean something and help you find the girls."

"We'll check it out…" Alex said as the phone went quiet, losing the connection. She tried to call Candice back but only got a recording.

Chapter Twelve
Alex

I called Skye's home number and her father answered. I explained the call I received from Ryan's mother.

"I'm sorry detective, my mother and Skye are in North Carolina on the Cherokee Indian Reservation. It is somewhat primitive and in some areas it's hard to get a signal. I'll have her call you if I hear from her."

I thanked him and hung up. "North Carolina? Well that was odd; she didn't mention she was going to North Carolina when they were in the office this morning." I said, mumbling to myself. I called dispatch and had them run the plate as I headed out the door.

If she's in North Carolina, how could she know about them being at a rest area...? Reservation...? I have to consider what she told me, but this is crazy. They seemed like honest and legitimate people. This is just too bazaar. Right now I have to go pick up Connie, maybe she will be able to shed some light on this.

ANN KIDWELL

Chapter Thirteen
<u>Skye</u>

Grammie came back from calling the detective. "Skye sweetie, our connection was cut short, but I believe I was able to get her the information. I just hope she believed me."

The nap had refreshed us all and we were listening attentively as Takena went on to explain many of the ways of the Cherokee. "Cherokees believe that the people are one with nature. The river, referred to as the *long man,* is a vital part of many things we give thanks for. The forest, especially the cedar tree, is revered and sacred. Whenever one takes from the earth, one leaves a token and says a prayer of thanks. When a Cherokee kills a deer for food, a prayer of thanks is said for the deer for giving its life to provide us with meat, and a little water is poured in its mouth to help it on its journey to the afterlife (West)."

Grammie joined in the explanation, "Here, material things are not as important as honoring Mother Earth. The Earth is referred to as the 'Mother.' It's a magical place indeed as you both will see."

Grammie went to the door and opened it to look out as the sun was setting. "Skye, Aaron, come quickly, I want you to see something," she called anxiously. "Look," she points to the small fireflies flashing on and off. "Here we call them lightning bugs." She said

"Wow, those are real?" I say, having never seen one before. "I thought those were only at Disneyland, I didn't know they were real. Why don't we have those in Washington?"

"I don't know little one, I wish we did, because I really miss them," she said.

Our arrival had missed the yearly gathering of the clans. A three day Pow Wow, wherein the Cherokee clans came together in remembrance of their survival of the Trail of Tears and their celebration of life's coexistence with Mother Earth. Grammie said she wanted her grandchildren to one day see the Pow Wow celebrations, but this was not the time. Now, the urgent focus was for me to learn about my gift and how to use that gift.

We all went outside to see the lightning bugs, and Aaron saw what looked like a campfire about a football field away from Takena's house. He pointed to it and asked if they were camping outside. Takena said that was the central fire and they would burn it year round, a tribal tradition. She encouraged him to go and introduce himself as many of the Cherokee men spent hours telling stories around the fire. "We have a lot of catching up to do, your Grammie and I, so you and Skye feel free to look around and explore your new surroundings. I know it's getting dark, but I'll leave the porch light on for you."

***

Candice

I linked arms with Takena as we made our way back inside to the kitchen. "I'm sorry it took so long for me to come back and visit and for you to meet your eldest great-grandson."

"You have a fine grandson; he has my brother's strong jaw line and such piercing eyes. It is as if he is able to see inside your soul."

"Yes he does, Mother, he even carries himself like my uncle. I think he may be a little taller. If he wore his dark hair longer, you would see an even greater resemblance. Not in character with his dark features, his intense light blue eyes penetrated your heart," Candice said, giving her mother a squeeze. "Maybe he will grace us with a nice smile before we head home. He is so intense; he appears older than his 21 years, with puffy dark circles under his eyes. I believe that he is hiding his real self from us, so I hope this visit will help him heal from whatever is bothering him."

"Things have a way of working themselves out," Takena said, placing a kiss on my forehead brushing away the worry lines.

Chapter Fourteen
<u>Alex</u>

After receiving the phone call from *The Polaris Project*, I grabbed my partner and headed to pick up Connie. Before I left the building, I received an urgent call from Candice Frost, Skye's Grandmother, with information about a rest area in that general direction. I quickly wrote down the information, but we were disconnected before I could ask where she received the information.

As soon as I could verify that Connie was truly one of the girls I was looking for, I would call Rita, Connie's mother, and let her know she was safe.

I drove over seventy miles to the restaurant hoping to find both girls, even though the call center said that only Connie was there. At least Connie may know where Becca is.

From my training and experience, I still felt this was more than a runaway. I've been operating on the assumption that the girls, Becca, in particular, were lured by a sophisticated predator. Becca could still be in the hands of a pedophile, or a trafficker, or both.

Finding Connie had brought this case back on the front burner just as we were running out of clues. There was no time to waste, I need to act quickly. It's about an hour to the restaurant. With lights and sirens, we should be able to cut that down. I needed to talk to anyone at that restaurant that might know how she got there and if they saw anything.

Did they leave Connie, or did she escape? Regardless, the guy would get as far away from her as he could, making him prone to go into hiding, and harder to find. I didn't want to waste any time. In the pit of my stomach, I felt Becca would soon be out of reach.

Thank God, one of them had turned up safe.

We arrived at the restaurant and found a middle aged couple had been keeping her safe until we arrived. The lady, Brenda, said she found her in the bathroom crying. Connie looked so young and exhausted. I thanked Brenda and her husband, and took Connie to our car and headed back to Lynnwood.

Before we started the car, I asked Connie, "Do you know where Becca is?"

"No, I ran away from them at a rest stop and hid in the back of Brenda's truck."

"A rest stop?" I had Mrs. Frosts' strange telephone call just before we left the office in my head. "Is that where Becca is?" I asked.

"Yes, she was there with Keilan and his sister, Mandy."

"What were they driving?"

"It was a new green GMC Denali truck. At least that's what Keilan said, I don't know much about trucks. He said it was new. I thought about getting the plate number, but I couldn't see the plate from the back of Brenda's truck."

"Is there anything else you can tell me? Where he lives and where were you guys going?"

"I don't know, Keilan said it was a surprise and he mentioned a house on the beach."

I got on the radio and put out an all points bulletin on a new green GMC Denali, and on the subjects known as Keilan and Mandy with a young runaway girl with them.

Connie was able to verify some of the information that I received from Mrs. Frost.

She had escaped from a rest area and they were in a new, green GMC Denali truck. Upon that verification, the detective had enough to issue an Amber alert with Becca's picture and the artist's rendition of Keilan. Also, units of the State Patrol were on their way to the rest area. I prayed they would get there in time.

Chapter Fifteen
Skye

I woke and dawn was just breaking. Grammie and Takena were busy making biscuits and gravy and I could smell the bacon. The weather was a little cooler, but the humidity made me feel sticky. Aaron had grabbed a biscuit and said he was going out to check things out. I took a quick bath and put on some shorts and tied my hair up.

When breakfast was ready, we sat around the table and talked about what would be in store for us for the next couple of days.

We were going to take a tour of this part of the reservation and go to the Oconaluftee Visitor Center so we could see the history of the tribe and learn about many of the Cherokee ways. We would have lunch at the casino, then return home for a rest, before having a light supper. Takena was spry for her age, but as Grammie put it, ninety is still ninety. After supper, Takena would decipher my dream and perform my naming ceremony. Takena would explain everything as we went along.

I found out from listening to Takena talking over breakfast that although this reservation is more prosperous with the casinos and it now has a visitor's center, the people are the same. Grammie said she feels the spirits of the forefathers and they seem to surround it all.

"Takena, what is the drumming I hear?" I asked, as she guided us down a path toward a circle with a small fire.

"Oh, I am so used to the sound; I forget to explain it to visitors. We have a tribe member that loves the central fire. When weather permits, he will keep it stoked and burning softly. He feels it brings a semblance of the old Cherokee ways, along with him softly beating the drum. In the evenings the elders will gather around the fire and tell stories that have been handed down through the generations. If we have time this evening, we will come out and sit and listen," she said softly. I saw a smile adorn her face, and she appeared to be lost in her memories. I reached down and place my hand in her small hand and she squeezed it and refocused on the here and now.

We moved around the area and saw the peaceful forest that was thick with trees and she pointed out trails leading toward a couple of bustling streams. The 21st century had barely touched this part of the reservation. There were the necessary electrical and plumbing features – but little else. It was off the main thoroughfare where there are many tourist attractions.

In keeping with the customs on the reservation, there were brightly costumed Cherokees with feathered head dresses and leather fringed trousers and skirts. These were being put away, but some of the participants still remained to play the steady beat of the drums, *the drums from my dreams*. The central ceremonial fire was ebbing in the center of a giant circle. Painted faces and bodies were being wiped clean and the adornment of beads, feathers, and beautiful outfits were being placed in boxes for the next ceremony.

"Many of the costumes are used in the *Unto These Hills*, a drama that has been put on by the Cherokee for over 60 years," said Takena when she saw me looking at the brightly colored costumes. I was in awe of the energy coursing through this beautiful place in the peaceful Smoky Mountains. Even Aaron's serious face relaxed and, for the first time, Grammie mentioned seeing a calm gentleness come to his features which she said she hadn't seen since he was a very young child.

The homes were modest single-story styled constructed homes and many were in disrepair with just the barest of essentials. We were greeted with smiles and a warm welcome. It was a much slower pace than I was used to. And I noticed the absence of electronic devices. People were talking to each other and seemed to be laughing and happy. We got to see the Tuckasegee River and some people on inner-tubes were traveling down it. We headed back to the car to go to the visitor's center then to lunch at the casino.

Takena loved talking about the Cherokee's ways, and continued, "Just two days ago, our annual Pow Wow ended with the revelry of dancing to the beat of the native drums and singing age old chants around an open fire to honor our Mother Earth. This is a reflective and humbling sight. Pow Wow's are held at many Native American Tribes across this great country and ours is always around the Fourth of July." She went on to explain that hearts were laid open and challenged and the Great Spirit visited our people during these colorful ceremonies.

She went on. "Although the different North American Tribes warred among themselves when the Europeans came to America more than 600 years ago, within the last 100 years they have united for one cause - to preserve their heritage and their way of life." You could tell she loved giving a voice to the Cherokee. She just beamed.

"In the Cherokee tribe, the elders are revered and sought out for their wisdom, guidance, and knowledge which had been passed from one generation to another through the telling of stories. The Cherokee is a matriarchal society, meaning the women of the tribes are looked up to and are part of making many of the important decisions." Takena chattered away, glowing. I looked at Grammie and she had a wide smile on her face. She was navigating us through the increasing traffic as we were getting to the main part of the Town of Cherokee.

I felt at ease immediately, but couldn't understand the other feelings that bombarded me. I have always felt more comfortable standing in the shadows since my shyness overwhelms me around strangers, so I tend to study people at great length before interacting with them. But here, I am immediately drawn to the tender, brown wrinkled face of my Great Grandmother. I have a very familiar feeling or memory of being held by her and hearing a melody sung in a language I didn't understand.

Takena had said that even though the revelry of the Pow Wow still lingered in the air, my journey was foremost as it was foretold in a dream two days prior to our arriving.

We arrived at the cultural center and were guided through some of the exhibits where women were weaving baskets and stringing beads. There was finger weaving with present day yarns and some with dyed yarns from the past. There was so much to see and learn that I couldn't take it all in. We only spent a couple of hours going through the live museum and Takena was looking tired. Grammie noticed and suggested we head to the Casino for lunch. Takena said their food was good and affordable, as the Casino's money was made in the gambling and shows.

I didn't expect the Casino to be so large. It was the tallest building in the area. The Casino had a hotel attached and a theater, but Grammie parked close to the entrance so Takena wouldn't have to walk so far.

We had a great lunch with some Southern food. "Come on, Skye, try some of the catfish and hush puppies," Grammie said.

"What are hush puppies?" I giggled at the name.

"They are small balls of deep fried cornbread with a hint of onions in them. They go well with fish."

I laughed. "Is everything deep fried in the South?"

"Pretty much," she said smiling. She enjoyed showing us this part of her heritage.

We finished our lunch and headed back to Takena's. With jet lag from the flight and being busy since yesterday, we were all feeling tired, especially Grammie and Takena.

It didn't take much for us to go to our respective beds and pallets for an afternoon nap. The doors and windows were open, letting a breeze flow through the house along with some box fans. The air was heavy with humidity which made it sticky for napping, but lying underneath the fans helped. The symphony of the birds chirping and the low rhythm of the drums lulled me to sleep.

Chapter Sixteen
<u>Skye</u>

We were all awake from our nap. Takena sat down at the table with me and took my hand in hers. "Skye, I am leaving to go prepare the wigwam for our ceremony tonight."

"What's a wigwam, Takena?"

"It is a dwelling the Cherokee used to live in and at times it is used as a sweat lodge. There are a few left on the reservation besides the ones at the museum. Remember the structure that was made from bent saplings in a dome shape with mud on the outsides? There is one just past the ceremonial fire we went to earlier. We make use of it quite often for different ceremonies."

"I remember."

"I will come and get you when I'm ready, okay? Oh, and as tempting as the fry bread looks, you will be fasting until tomorrow night, okay?"

"Yes, I'll wait," I said. I did remember the wigwam at the museum and it was round and had a chimney in the center and they said they were used more in the winter months when it would get really cold. I was just surprised that they had them outside of the museum.

Takena was back in about a half hour. She sat down at the table and began talking about my first naming ceremony.

Grammie had explained on the plane that a Cherokee is given a name within seven days of their birth. If the child is a girl, she is usually named by the grandmother. If it is a boy, a trusted male figure will name him. Later, when they are grown or accomplish something unique to them, their name may change to one more appropriate to their character. "I believe that you have come to the time when your Cherokee name will be changed to one more in line with your gift." She said.

Takena picked up the conversation. "Since your gift has shown itself to be the gift of sight, you will be instructed what that means and what purpose it will serve."

I enjoyed listening to how I received my name, *Skye*. Grammie relayed the story while looking at me. "Because you were born in Japan, your formal naming ceremony was performed when you were three months old after you came to the States with your parents. Takena, as the Wise Woman of the Wolf Clan, had blessed you in this first naming ceremony. She took you from my arms and passed you over the sacred fire and dipped you in the flowing stream called the 'Long Man.' The elements of fire and water were considered gifts from the Great Spirit. Fire symbolized the division of man from the animal kingdom, as only man can kindle and maintain fire. Moving water symbolized purity and strength of an individual. As is the custom, I got to choose your name. I chose to name you Skye, which is Cherokee and means "reflection." Takena will take you now and prepare you for your new name.

Takena took my hand and walked me a short distance to a clearing where a small ceremonial fire burned near a small wigwam structure with an animal skin stretched across the opening.

She explained, "I cleared the sacred place earlier in preparation for you. Now I must prepare you."

"Stand tall and I will perform a cleansing ritual of smudging to clear the negative energy which may have attached to you." She explained, "This is done to prepare you to enter this sacred space."

The smudging began when Takena took an abalone shell and filled it with a wrapping of sweet grass, sage, and cedar. She lit it and just as it started to burn, the flame was snuffed out. As she worked she explained, "When performing this ceremony in an abalone shell, the vibration of all four elements: earth, fire, air, and water are present. The herbs are from the earth, the burning of these herbs represents fire, the shell represents water, and the smoke represents the air. When these four elements come together, it enhances the ceremony. The powerful herbs are used to cleanse away the darkness from the spirit and to open up the spirit to enlightenment." Takena had explained to me how the smudging was done, then she proceeded. A prayer was offered to the Great Spirit to guide her hands, after which it was customary to ask permission from me to proceed, even though I had given it by being here. With affirmation from me, she began.

The resulting smoke was fanned toward me with a hawk's feather, beginning at my toes and proceeding up the front of my body in a symbolic ritual of freeing the spirit within. The smoke was then drawn down my back to the ground to symbolize the anchoring of my physical body to Mother Earth. I don't know how long the ceremony took. I felt adrift and only became aware of my surroundings when Takena placed her gentle hand back on my shoulder.

The smoke was pleasant and I breathed in a multitude of smells from the forest, the warm mist and the smudging smoke. When I closed my eyes during the prayer, I found myself watching the ceremony as if from afar. Hearing the chant from Takena which resonated throughout the ceremony sounded familiar in my mind along with a soft drumming in the background.

Grammie and Aaron left the sacred ground as the rest of the ceremony would be between Takena and me.

After the smudging, Takena gave me a small cup of liquid to drink. "It is just called 'Black Drink,' she said. Takena told me she had picked the leaves and branches of the yaupon holly bush this morning and then they were lightly dried in a clay pot over the fire. Much like coffee, the roasting made the caffeine soluble. After browning, they are boiled in a large container of water until the liquid reaches a dark brown or black color, giving it its name. Then it was strained into a cup to cool just enough to drink. She said it is a ritual drink and its effect is stronger when hot.

I drank it and then was given a drink of water to rinse my mouth. It wasn't unpleasant. Takena directed me to an animal skin on the ground of the wigwam and told me to lie down to sleep and dream. The temperature inside of the wigwam was much cooler and drier than outside so I drifted off to sleep easily. It felt like a heavy load had been lifted from me. I'm not sure how long I slept but my dream was vivid. Upon waking I sat quietly near the door with my eyes shut keeping my breathing small as Takena had instructed. Within a few minutes, she was back.

She guided me out into the open air and directed me to sit upon the ground around the fire. It appeared to be twilight and the sun was just setting. She brushed the hair out of my eyes and asked, "Skye, my child, tell me about your dream?"

"My dream was very vivid and I remember the details as if they were real. Was that from the black drink?"

She smiled at the question. "Yes, the black drink does help, but you will find that your dreams will be more vivid due to your gift, and the vision quest tomorrow will answer many of your questions."

"Now tell me about your dream." she patted my hands and encouraged me to speak.

"Well, it's hard to put into words. I don't know what it means, but it is a breezy day in the meadow where I see myself with my eyes closed and I hear the music of the wind. I am compelled to dance. My dream has eyes that watch from above in circles and circles and sees that there is magic in the dance. I am wearing a headband around my forehead that has a third eye of wisdom with a black and white feather with blue and red beads strung on it near my right ear. As I spin and balance, I hold out my arms I am dancing, but also viewing myself from high above as though my spirit is flying outside of myself. I don't know how to explain it."

"That is for me to interpret for you. This is the grace of a warrior's dance. This comes to you through the Great Spirit that you will have the gift of sight and shall be called Nunnehi (nun-NAH-he), which means Graceful Warrior. This is your Cherokee name and all who hear this will know that what you see, you will speak as the truth. Have no doubts in your gift as it will at times be a burden, but has a purpose. This you need to trust. More will be revealed at your vision quest tomorrow."

Chapter Seventeen
Aaron

I hadn't heard the voices in my head since I'd been here. It's the longest I've gone without hearing them. Not hearing the voices made me realize how much they interfered with my thinking and made me anxious. It was so peaceful and quiet, but also different as I had lived with them for so long. This morning, all I heard were the birds and what sounded like tree frogs.

After leaving the cultural center, we headed back home. I was exhausted and fell quickly to sleep on my pallet beneath the fan. An hour later, I awoke refreshed and wanted to explore the reservation and hike through the woods. Inspired by the cultural center, I wanted to see more. I grabbed a biscuit off of the stove, donned my hat, planted a kiss on Grammie's cheek, and headed out.

I hiked some of the trails and crossed a couple of streams of crystal clear water where you could count the pebbles on the bottom. I saw people fishing and kids sliding down rocks into the water. The waters were clear and cold. Then I found myself back at the central fire and sat around and listened to some of the elders exchange stories again. They welcomed my questions and I felt accepted. They told stories that had been handed down from their fathers and when they spoke to each other in Cherokee, I didn't understand. They said they would teach me their language if I was going to stay longer.

Grammie came to the central fire and asked me to come with her as she wanted me to witness a cleansing ceremony that Takena does. It was the smudging ceremony on Skye. Takena explained what the different herbs were used for and what the significance of the ceremony was. It was magical.

After the cleansing ceremony, Grammie and I went back to sit around the fire. Skye's dreaming interpretation and naming ceremony would be done with only Takena and Skye present.

Meeting and listening to Takena and the history of my ancestors, I wanted to learn as much as I could.

I was filled with such a rush of emotion. The feeling of hopelessness was lifted and the cloud which I'd been carrying disappeared.

I cried. I don't know why, but I couldn't help it. Grammie cradled me in her arms and hummed a Cherokee healing song. When I pulled away from her she said, "There is no shame in crying; it cleans the spirit." No longer self-conscious, I broke down, letting all those years of keeping my secret and feeling out of place dissolve with the realization that I belonged here. To me, this felt like home.

The steady beat of the drum lulled me and I closed my eyes. Grammie tapped me on the shoulder and offered me a refreshing dipper of water.

It was time to pull her aside and tell her what I had been hiding from everyone. "Grammie, I've been hearing voices and I haven't told anyone because I thought I might be crazy. Do you think it could be a Cherokee gift?"

"Oh Aaron, how long has this been going on?"

"Since my junior year in high school."

"What kind of voices? Were they telling you to do things, I don't understand?"

"They didn't seem to be directed to me, but conversations of people talking when there wasn't anyone around. I would hear a child crying and asking God to help his mommy. They didn't make sense and I didn't recognize them."

"Is it always a child's voice or are the voices always different?"

"It is usually a man and woman's voice and they are fighting, but when I first heard them, there was a baby in the background. Then as the years went by, it seemed like I could hear the baby begin to talk. The last I heard, the little boy was crying and begging daddy not to hurt mommy."

"I wish you had told me. I will speak to Takena to see what she says. When was the last time you heard them?"

"The night before last."

With that, she gave me a hug and patted my back and cooed to me. "Everything will be alright; you'll see. Everything will be alright."

Chapter Eighteen
Becca

"I had no idea that Connie was going to run off, honest." I pleaded. I could tell Keilan didn't believe me. The look he gave her was scary and for the first time, I felt fear when looking at him. *What have I done?*

"You bitch," Keilan said to Mandy. "I give you one thing to do and you screw that up. Keep an eye on the girls and make sure they don't call home, and you let one escape? She couldn't have gotten far. Check around and see if you can find her, and take Becca with you. You better damn well find her. Do it now!" he yelled. "I've got some calls to make.

Oh my God, I can't believe that is the same Keilan I've been talking to on the phone. I'm scared. I can't quit shaking.

Mandy and I checked in the restroom stalls and by the vending machines, calling her name, but we were unable to find her.

As I walked around the rest area looking for Connie, I was wondering what I had gotten myself into. Looking down, I noticed a large white feather with spots of black on it. I moved to pick it up as Mandy came up behind me.

"What did you find? Did you spot something of Connie's?" Mandy asked.

"No, it's just a feather. I heard that if you see a feather, it means that angels are around you."

"Well, that's a load of shit. I don't believe in angels," Mandy said. "Now we better find Connie, or we will both regret it. Where would she go? I thought you two were besties?"

"We are, it's just that she was missing her mom. Maybe she went to borrow a phone so she could call her mother," I said, hoping to create a good excuse for why she wasn't in the bathroom.

"Shit, shit…boy will Keilan be pissed. That's why he took your phones. Do you want your mother to stop this wedding? That's what will happen if they find you. Oh fuck, we are screwed now." Mandy grabbed my arm as I reached down and picked up the feather.

We both headed back to the truck.

"Becca thinks she may have gone to borrow a phone so she could call her mother," Mandy told Keilan.

"Now that's not going to happen. You better find her and be ready to go as soon as you do, or you will pay. What the hell were you thinking?" Keilan's anger caught me off guard. He was never like this on the phone.

What have you done, Connie? You are ruining everything. Everything was going so good until you had to mess it up.

I was angry at Connie for making Keilan mad. If she had just listened to me, everything would have been okay, and we would be on our way to the coast.

Still unable to find her, we returned to the truck and Keilan grabbed Mandy's arm. He turned her toward him and with a closed fist, hit her in the face and knocked her to the ground. A woman came around the restroom building and saw Mandy on the ground and Keilan standing astride her.

"Hey!" the woman yelled. "What are you doing? Is she okay?"

"Mind your own fucking business, bitch. If she wasn't falling down drunk we wouldn't be stuck here," Keilan growled at the stranger. "Now get your drunk ass in the truck and let's go." Keilan grabbed Mandy's arm and directed her toward the truck.

"Becca, grab her other arm and help me get her inside." I pulled her into the front seat as Keilan pushed from the outside.

Mandy began to regain consciousness.

I sat between Keilan and Mandy. I touched Mandy's eye where it was swelling. "You didn't need to hit her. Even I didn't know Connie was going to leave."

"Shut up, bitch, or I'll give you some of what Mandy got," Keilan said, pulling out of the rest area.

Mandy touched my arm to get my attention and shook her head side to side. She placed her index finger to her lips, indicating, 'silence.' I understood.

I'm so confused. What is Keilan doing? What am I doing? Where is Connie? I'm afraid if we do find her, Keilan might hurt her. She must have seen this in Keilan. This has got to be some kind of mistake. We're going to be married.

If I just give it some time and Keilan calms down everything will be okay.

"We can't risk waiting around here any longer. Mandy keep an eye out and let me know if you see her." Keilan commanded as we pulled out of the rest area.

I looked up at the stormy sky and I spotted a large white bird as it circled above. It made me remember the big owl I'd seen in the tree, just this morning. It seemed like a lifetime ago.

Keilan turned an angry scowl at Mandy. "You just fucked us. How could you let her get away? Anymore slip-ups and I will find a replacement for you. I will bury your body so no one will ever find you. You know I mean it. Now we have to switch vehicles soon, just in case Connie goes to the police."

I felt a chill go through Mandy. She was shaking.

"She won't go to the cops. She has no idea what's really happening. She just thinks you and Becca are going to get married. She'll probably just call her mother. She doesn't know your real name and as many backstreets as you were taking; she couldn't tell where we were. Besides, she thinks you are going to California to get married on the beach. She will never know we aren't even heading in that direction," Mandy said, pleading nervously, trying to redeem herself.

***

Keilan

I just pulled out of the rest area and headed south again. I drove for about an hour when an Amber Alert with Becca's and my description came over my phone.

"Damn it to hell, they have a description of the truck. We've got to get off the highway." Taking the next exit, I circled back and headed north, but on side roads.

A call just came in from Mason. "Keilan, you've fucked up. Weaver just got the Amber Alert. You need to fix this, man. Head to the cabin and Weaver has another vehicle for you to use. The Denali will be scrubbed. Weaver said if you get caught, you better keep your mouth shut or you're a dead man. Are you getting this?"

"Yeah, I get it. You know I would never roll on Weaver. We're headed to the cabin now."

The phone disconnected.

Damn that bitch. Mandy will pay for that mistake! Damn!

Chapter Nineteen
__Alex__

I took Connie back to the Lynnwood Police Department where her mother would pick her up in a few hours. I'd questioned her a little on the ride back to the station, but her eyes were puffy from crying and she'd withdrawn when I told her that her mother was on the way. A few minutes later she was sound asleep.

We got back to the office just as the sun was beginning to set. It had been a long day. Jeff went to get dinner for Connie and while we waited, I took her into one of the interview rooms so I could record the questioning for later review.

"Okay Connie, do you feel comfortable answering some questions for me? Do you mind if we start at the beginning?"

"Yeah, that's okay."

"Do you know the guy's full name that contacted Becca online?"

Connie looked down at her hands and seemed hesitant to answer. "Um, can I have a Kleenex? My nose is running. Um, Keilan, but I don't know the last name. It sounded Italian. San... something."

"What else do you know about him? Did you meet his mother or father?"

"No, but we met his sister, Mandy. Keilan took us to her house from the airport. We didn't stay long. Keilan wanted her to take us shopping at a mall. He told her to get us lots of clothes. He said they were for their wedding."

"Okay, go on."

"Mandy said Keilan liked stilettos. That was when I started to get a creepy feeling."

"What do you mean?"

"Becca and I are 14, what do we need stilettos for? I'm from Detroit and I've seen lots of hookers wearing stilettos. That just started to creep me out."

"Do you know where the mall was?"

"No, I didn't pay attention to the name, but it was big."

"What were some of the stores, if you can remember?"

"Umm, lots of small clothing stores, but there was a Victoria's Secret; that is where Mandy wanted to go. She said Becca needed some sexy nighties for her wedding. Keilan was planning a surprise for her. That's where we were going this morning."

"Do you know what that surprise was?"

"No, but Becca thought we were going to the coast or California. She said that Keilan was rich, but his sister's house wasn't rich. At least it didn't look rich to me. It didn't have much furniture or anything. The walls were bare."

"Well, that was a good observation. So what made Becca think he was rich?"

"He drove a new truck and told Becca that he worked with his dad and they made lots of money working for rich people. I think it was some kind of landscaping business that they were partners in."

I'm busy making notes and Connie seems to be opening up a little, she's making more eye contact and seems to be relaxing a little.

"What made you and Becca run away?"

"Becca had a fight with her Mom, because she was too strict with her and she monitored everything she did. She said her mother treated her like a baby. She threatened to take away her phone."

"How did you get the plane tickets?"

"Keilan had the tickets waiting for us at the airport, and he arranged for us to meet a friend of his in Detroit who drove us to the airport."

"Do you know who that was?"

"No, but she was older, maybe 40."

The phone buzzed "The food had arrived." The voice over the intercom said.

"Good, we'll take a break and be right out. Connie, do you think you can eat anything. I know you had lunch at the restaurant but I believe I heard your tummy growl a little bit ago."

That brought a smile to her face which made her look so young. She brushed her hair behind her ear and followed me out the door.

"Can I use the bathroom first?"

I pointed down the hall, "It's right down there, the door on your left."

"Thanks."

When she came out of the restroom, we headed to the break room where Jeff had left the takeout sandwiches. I handed her a sandwich and soda. "Do you mind if I leave you in here for awhile? I need to make some phone calls?"

"No, that's okay, I'm good."

I stepped out of the room, and directed some follow-up things for Jeff to do. "Run all the variations of Keilan San... and Mandy San... through the databases to see if we get some hits. Also, check any landscaping companies that sound Italian. I know it's a long shot, but it's all we have."

A few phone calls and about 15 minutes later, I headed back to the break room.

"Well, Connie, did you get enough to eat?"

"Yeah, I love BLT's."

"Okay, are you ready to answer a few more questions?"

"Yes. When is my mom going to be here?"

"In about an hour, I've sent an officer to pick her up."

"Was she really mad?"

"She sounded relieved."

"Really?" Connie asked.

"Yeah, she did. I think maybe she was scared for you. Do you mind going back to the interview room?"

"No, that's fine. Am I in trouble for running away."

"Not at the moment with the police. We are more relieved that you have been found safe. Your mom may ground you or something. You don't need to worry about that now, okay?"

"Okay."

We headed back to the interview room and I pushed the record button. "Now do you remember anything about Mandy's house besides it being sparsely furnished? What was the color and was it on a busy street?"

"No, it was down some winding roads and not many neighbors. The houses were spread apart. It was a two-tone green. The grass was weedy and dead."

"Go on, anything else you can remember?"

"Becca said she saw a white owl. Do you have any owls around here? I didn't see it, but Becca said it was the biggest owl she had ever seen."

"Hmm, we have lots of owls around here so that doesn't help much. Was it far from the airport? How long did it take you to get there?"

"It took maybe a half an hour. We were chatting with Keilan, so I wasn't paying much attention to the time."

"Okay, is there anything else you can think of to add? What made you decide to get away from Keilan?"

"Well, last night he asked Becca, if I was a virgin. That was another thing that creeped me out. The way he was looking at me in the rearview mirror, it was a warning stare. Cold. I was afraid. I begged Becca to come with me, but she wouldn't. She said I was ruining everything."

Connie began to cry. "I wish she had come with me. Are you going to find her?" she asked between sobs. "I didn't want to leave her, but she wouldn't listen to me."

I got up and hugged her. "That's enough for now. Your mom should be here shortly. Is there anything I can get for you? Do you need to go to the restroom? I think the soda is going right through me."

"Yeah, me too." She giggled, and we went to the bathroom, then I brought her back to the break room so she could relax a little.

I headed to my desk to see what Jeff had found. "This Keilan guy is giving me the creeps. Have you found anything?"

"No, all dead ends. What about you?"

"I believe this guy is a predator, he wanted to know if Connie was a virgin. So I think he is trafficking in young girls. We've got to find Becca."

There was some commotion from the entryway. Connie's mother, Rita had arrived at the Lynnwood Police Department. I hadn't been prepared for the hostile and extremely annoyed woman. Rita carried a hard severe look and appeared much older than her 36 years. She was thin and garish looking with lots of mascara around the eyes and a thin set mouth with a missing tooth on the bottom front. She had a sallow jaundice complexion from years of smoking, and a possible alcohol or drug addiction, if I guessed correctly. She was uncooperative and unwilling to answer any questions, although she asked before leaving, "Am I going to be reimbursed for my airline ticket and expenses? Ya know, victims compensation or whatever it's called. I don't have money to be flying all over the place chasing her ass."

I sat her down and tried to fill her in on Connie's escape and that we were still hunting for Becca, but Rita wasn't listening.

She grabbed Connie's arm and said, "I know you ran away to just go whoring around, and you're not, I repeat not going to cooperate with the police because they can't be trusted. They can't be trusted. You learn real quick, young lady, that you can go from bein' the victim to bein' a suspect in a heartbeat."

"Mrs. Young, can I get you some coffee? I would like to ask Connie some more questions."

"No. She ain't answering no more of your damn questions. Now, get someone to take us to the airport, I need to get home. I had to borrow the money to get here. If you ain't found out enough, then there isn't any more to say. C'mon Connie, let's go. Becca's mother can worry about her. I knew you were going to get in trouble with that girl."

Connie looked at me and then cast her eyes to the floor. Her spirit was broken and now she was at the mercy of her mother. Even if Connie wanted to help, there wasn't any more she could tell us with her mother here. I hoped some of the information Connie provided would help us get Becca back home.

Before Connie was safely turned over to her mother, she had remembered that Keilan drove a dark green GMC Denali. She didn't know the license plate number.

Mrs. Frost had furnished the license plate number when she'd called, but the plate had been stolen off another pickup a couple of weeks before. I was able to issue an Amber Alert with a picture of Becca and the detailed drawing of Keilan and the description of the truck with the stolen plates on it. At least that was something.

Chapter Twenty
Aaron

The following day, when Skye went on her vision quest, Grammie came to me, "Aaron, I spoke with Takena about the voices and I explained to her that you seemed to be hearing a conversation and a child's voice. She said that you may be manifesting the Cherokee gift of "hearing" and that she would like you to stay here with her. Is that something you would be willing to do?"

"Really?"

"Yes, Aaron. She could teach you the Cherokee ways and you would be here to help her. Would that work for you?"

"What about my belongings and clothes and stuff at Dad's?"

"We can work that out later. You can send a list to your dad of what you need and he can send it to you in the mail. Can you live without cell service or gaming?"

"I have for the last couple of days. At first I missed it, but sitting around the central fire and listening to the elders and the sounds from the forest, that's better than any video game. If I miss it too much, I can make a trip into town. Someone is always going in."

"Sounds like you have it covered then," Grammie said, giving me a little hug and a patting like she does all the grandkids.

That something I'm going to miss.

I get to stay here. I never dreamed that my life would take this turn. The voices are a gift, not a curse! I'm so happy. My mind is racing a mile a minute with all the possibilities. I can help Takena and be here for her and she can teach me about the Cherokee ways and my gift.

My journey begins here, where I will be able to find my own calling.

ANN KIDWELL

Chapter Twenty-One
Nunnehi

I awoke the next morning rested and excited about my vision quest. Leaving Seattle seemed like a lifetime ago. I would have liked to stay longer but Grammie couldn't stay as she needed to be home with Grandpa. She promised that we would visit again soon.

I was still fasting so I watched Grammie make biscuits and gravy. She had a rhythm making the biscuits from scratch. She tried to teach me, but mine ended up looking like hockey pucks. She made it look effortless, almost like magic, and I found I was mesmerized watching the process.

When Takena and I returned from the dreaming and naming ceremony last evening, I excitedly told Grammie and Aaron about my new Cherokee name. I told them it was spelled Nunnehi, pronounced *nun-Nah-he* with the emphasis on the middle syllable. Takena explained that I would continue to use Skye during my normal life but would be referred to by Nunnehi when my gift was manifesting.

During breakfast, I continued to say the name over and over. I loved the sound of it. Between gorging himself on the biscuits and gravy, Aaron practiced pronouncing Nunnehi with me. He was the Aaron I knew when we were younger, less guarded and more relaxed. He even had the sparkle of mischief in his eyes. Apparently, this trip was a healing trip for him.

After breakfast, Takena took me on a hike along a trail to a small clearing in the trees in a cove high in the Smoky Mountains about two miles from the village. The forest was thick and lush with small trails meandering through the mountainous terrain. The air was heavy with the morning mist.

I wore a Cherokee dress that belonged to Takena. It was made from deer hide and embellished with beads sewn on by Takena before her own vision quest, many years before. My long black hair was in two braids with the ends wrapped in leather laces. Around my forehead was a beaded band with a third eye in the center, and over my right ear hung blue and red beads attached to a white and black feather.

Takena guided me on how I needed to prepare. "Pick a comfortable spot in which to begin, Nunnehi, and sit upon the forest blanket. Be comfortable, as you will be sitting for a while. Use all your senses. Look at your surroundings; hear the rustle of the leaves in the trees and the singing of the birds. Feel the sun upon your face, taste Mother Earth's pungent breathe on your tongue, and smell the cedars and mustiness of the forest floor. Close your eyes and experience all of these senses. Your mind will now visualize all that is out there."

She continued, "You will be visited by many animal spirit guides, but only one will choose you. Ask the Great Spirit to bring the chosen animal guide for you, and it will be so. When you have met your animal spirit guide, you will become the student and your guide will be your teacher and all your questions will be answered. The gift you have been given will be revealed through your lesson, so listen carefully, as your life will begin anew. When your animal spirit guide has chosen you, it will be with you forever and will come to you in your dreams and when there is a message or when you call." Takena placed a soft kiss upon my forehead then turned and walked away.

I left my eyes closed and allowed my senses to experience the surroundings. "Great Spirit, I am Nunnehi and I am here to receive your instruction and to become one with my animal spirit guide," I whispered to the soft wind in the quiet of the forest. I listened to the rustle of leaves and the crunching of twigs and branches as a forest creature foraged for food. The *Long Man* bubbled over rocks and pebbles.

I opened my eyes and the first animal to come to my thoughts was the Fox. Fox spoke to me. "I have the ability to blend with the forest and seem to disappear. My abilities are cunning; observation; sure-footedness; camouflage; and adaptability. With fox medicine, you will be taught the art of Oneness. I am not your spirit animal, but in times I may work together with your spirit animal."

"Thank you, Fox, for coming to me. I look forward to witnessing your gifts someday."

Then the Deer came and told me, "I am Deer and I will teach you the power of gentleness of spirit to heal all wounds. I will teach you to melt the hearts of demons and replace your fears with love." I felt drawn to the love of Deer, but I knew Deer was not my animal spirit guide.

The third animal to come was the White Owl. "Nunnehi, I am called Night Eagle and am associated with clairvoyance. I can see what others cannot. With Owl medicine, no one can deceive you with your keen insight. Through me you can see. Graceful Warrior, we are on a journey to right the deeds that have gone wrong. If we can work together, we can save some of the downtrodden." I felt instantly the truth the owl spoke. "I am your eyes at great distances, and I have sent you visions while you sleep. Know that it is time. We do not seek this war, but we do not shy from it either."

The White Owl continued, "Many years ago, before the Trail of Tears, the white man and warring tribes would take young Cherokee women and sell them as slaves at auctions. Be it known, this is still happening to all peoples. Our Mother Earth cries. Slavery is an unjust war that preys on the weak and vulnerable. Your quest is to teach and be a protector of all whom are victims. Heed your visions and dreams. Know that they come from me. Together we will make a difference."

Hours had passed and the sun dipped in the western sky. I felt a purpose and oneness with the land. Aware that although the time spent here had been short, I am needed elsewhere. I brushed the pine needles from my native dress and proceeded down the trail toward home.

When I got back to Takena's, she had set aside some of the fry bread and beans as she knew I
would be hungry and thirsty. We all talked for a little while, then Takena and Grammie went off to bed as we needed to get an early start for the airport in the morning.

Aaron and I talked late into the night. He had spent many hours sitting around the ceremonial fire and learning from the elders. He told me that he would be staying and helping Takena while learning more about the Cherokee ways. I saw a light shining in his eyes I hadn't seen for a long time. We talked more; then we both fell asleep.

Upon waking the next morning, Aaron told Takena, "I am so glad I'm staying here with you to learn the ways of the Cherokee. Last night has been the best sleep that I've had in many years. I don't feel that I'm ready to participate in any of the ceremonies, but I want to learn more about my heritage."

Takena's eyes sparkled with delight. "I was hoping you would agree to stay and learn the ways of your father's heritage."

Grammie gave Aaron a big hug and said that she was so happy that he had chosen to stay. "I was worried about you, but in Takena's hands and tutelage, you will come to know your destiny also. I will miss you though. But you can write me. You do remember how to write a letter, don't you?" she laughed, giving him a squeeze, referring to texting and cell phones.

We all exchanged hugs and tearful goodbyes. Then Grammie and I
headed   home.

Chapter Twenty-Two
<u>Becca</u>

We had just gotten off the highway when Keilan pulled over and got out of the truck. He pulled me out and pushed me toward the backdoor of the vehicle and told me to get in and lay on the floor.

"Why?"

"It doesn't matter why, just get in and lie down."

Mandy threw a blanket over me and slid into the backseat. "If you know what's good for you, you'll stay quiet. Keilan doesn't like to be questioned."

"But I don't know what's going on," I whispered.

"Just shut up and be still, you will find out soon enough," Mandy pushed me down further to keep me from getting up and looking out the window.

Keilan's phone received a text message and after he read it he told Mandy, "Mason said that Weaver wasn't happy about the screwup. It wasn't my fucking screw-up. Damn you Mandy, you will pay. Shit rolls downhill."

After that things got quiet for a while and I don't know how long I was on the floor, but it seemed like forever. "Can I please get up?" I begged.

"No you can't." Keilan said, spitting out the words.

"But why? What have I done?"

"Mandy put a sock in her mouth, if she doesn't shut the fuck up," he said.

I didn't say another word. I was scared and didn't know what was happening. I didn't want to get hit in the face like Mandy had. Shaking uncontrollably, my stomach rolled. "I think I'm going to be sick," I whispered to Mandy.

She whispered back. "You better not fucking puke in Keilan's truck or we're both dead. You hear me?"

I nodded and swallowed the bile coming up in my throat.

A few minutes later, Keilan answered another call.

I couldn't hear the call because Keilan was wearing earbuds, but he told Mandy about the conversation.

"Mason said a silver Lexus is at the cabin and this truck will be cleaned. He also said that the other two packages will be delivered by the time we get there. The bidding is up to $3700 and the price will be more before the auction ends at six o'clock Friday evening. The price will soar once we get her picture posted."

"Okay." Mandy said, "How long until we get to the cabin, I gotta pee."

"We should be there in about 45 minutes."

"Well there goes our trip to the coast and you can thank Connie the cunt for that." Keilan said with a mocking tone. "I knew I didn't like that bitch. I'm not in the mood for anymore shit and the pretending is done, you hear that, Ms. Becca?"

"What did I do wrong?" I said, crying.

"Oh, baby, wait and you will see." He said again. "Just keep her quiet Mandy; I don't want to hear another peep out of her."

"Did you hear that, Mandy? The bidding on the virgins always gets top dollar and those sick sons-a-bitches are weird and want all kinds of extras. But they're going to love our little Becca," he said with a sick laugh.

Virgin. At that word panic rose in my chest and throat. *Keilan said he was glad I was still a virgin. Oh, dear God, it can't be me he's talking about. He loves me. He wants to marry me. He called me his "gift from Detroit." None of this makes sense.*

I started shaking again and I know Mandy felt it because she nudged me with her foot and mumbled, "You better shut up and pull it together or Keilan will make you pay."

We turned down a gravel road and slowed down. I couldn't hear any traffic outside. It was really quiet. It seemed like we'd been driving forever and Mandy kept pushing my head into the floor. Finally, the truck quit moving and Keilan turned it off.

The backdoor opened and Mandy nudged me. "Get up, we're here."

I sat up and the glare from the setting sun hurt my eyes. I was in the mountains somewhere a wilderness or forest with a cabin and a white van and Jeep parked at the side.

Before I could get my bearings, Mandy blindfolded me and transferred me to another car. Probably the Jeep I saw parked by the cabin as I could feel the stick shift and it felt like a jeep I had ridden in one once. She told me not to remove the blindfold or I would be sorry. "When we get to the destination, I will remove it."

When Mandy took the blindfold off, we were in a salon in someone's home where we met a friend of hers. "She needs a real makeover. Cut and straighten it, but make it look cute cause she's going to get her picture taken." Mandy said with a chuckle. "Oh, and let's make her a red head. The men really go for gingers."

"No, you can't cut my hair," I cried. "I don't want my hair cut or straightened."

"Well, you can thank your bestie for that. If your picture wasn't posted in an Amber Alert, you wouldn't have to."

"No." I grabbed the brush from the girl's hand. Mandy spun the chair around and slapped me across the face. "That's not your choice. Give her back the brush and sit still. It will be over before you know it."

It took about three hours from the time we got there until we were done. Mandy had to take me to the bathroom a couple of times as I started puking, but there wasn't much in my stomach so I had the dry heaves. Then she tied my arms to the chair and had the girl watch me while she went to get some sandwiches and soda because I was weak from not eating and she was afraid I would pass out.

She told the girl there would be a big tip in this, but she could never tell anyone.

"I get it. Mums the word," she said.

The girl just did the work and never said a word about herself or anything to give me a feel for who she was or what was going on.

"Tell me what's happening, what are you going to do to me?" I begged Mandy. *Why was I being tied up and blindfolded. What did I do wrong? My nose was running and my eyes were puffy and red, and I couldn't keep from shaking. My whole world changed when Connie left. Would they be doing this if Connie was still here?*

When she was done, I looked totally different. Mandy slipped the girl some money and reminded her to keep her mouth shut, and there would be more where that came from.

It was dark when we returned to the cabin. The truck was gone.

Keilan came out to the car and it was pitch black outside, until Keilan turned on a floodlight on the side of the cabin. Another light came on at one of the outbuildings. He told Mandy he was impressed with my transformation. I shook from fear and could hardly speak.

"Keilan, what did I do wrong?" I begged. "You said you loved me and now you are treating me like this," I began sobbing again.

Mandy grabbed my arm and pulled me around to the back of the cabin following Keilan. The shed with the light had doors on the side that open like an old outside entrance to a root cellar or cold storage shed. The doors had a padlock on them and Keilan opened it with a key.

"Get in there, Becca. I don't want to even look at you now." I pulled away from Mandy and ran in the opposite direction. Keilan grabbed me by the hair and yanked me back. He pulled me up face to face with him. "We aren't playing this little game anymore, your friend saw to that. So get your ass down in the cellar and keep your mouth shut. The client wants you bruise free, so don't make me hurt you."

I counted four stairs as I felt my way into the cellar. I heard the door shut and the padlock locking. It was pitch black and it smelled damp, but I heard breathing and crying, then a whisper. "Where are we? What are they going to do to us? The police are never going to find me in here." Heavy sobbing and wheezing echoed in the darkness.

I felt along the wall, running my fingers across bricks and dirt. It smelled musty like wet earth. I whispered, "Keep talking and I'll try to find you. Ouch!" I fell forward over something wooden, and my palm felt a leg jerk away. "I'm sorry, I fell over something." I said.

It sounded like a little child was crying. "I'm Becca. What's your name? Is there more than one person down here? I hear someone else breathing?" My hand was next to someone's leg. They were shaking and the sobbing was coming from the person I was closest to. "I wish I could see. How long have you been down here?" I tried again to get the person to talk to me. Their voices as they whispered to each other sounded young and scared.

"Jessica. My name is Jessica, and I'm with Tina. I'm 15 and so is Tina. We were shopping at the mall, then we got into a car with an older girl that we met there. She said she was going our way, then she said she just needed to stop and pick something up at Safeway. She pulled in next to a white van, and a couple of guys opened our door and pulled us into the van." The sobbing started again, and she tried to talk between crying. "Uh uh…" The girl sniffled. "It happened so fast, we didn't have time to scream or yell. They put tape over our mouths and tied our hands behind our backs and shoved us to the floor. One guy held a gun to Tina's head and said they would shoot her dead if we made any noise. Then we were brought here. It seemed like we were driving forever."

"Where are we? Do you know this area? I just got a glimpse when they took me from the car," I said.

"No, I don't recognize anything, but it's a ways from the mall, or at least it seemed like we were in that van for a long time," Jessica said.

The girls continued to talk about how they'd ended up here. "I'm so cold," said Jessica. We were crying, shivering, coughing, and praying to ourselves. Gradually exhaustion took over and everything was quiet.

I fell asleep in the cellar and dreamed of an Indian girl with white wings like an angel. She told me that the police were looking for me. The dream was peaceful and I wanted to stay asleep in that dream.

ANN KIDWELL

Chapter Twenty-Three
Alex

I received notification that two young blond fifteen-year-old girls were missing from a mall in Lynnwood. They were last seen getting into a car with a woman about 19 or 20. A security camera in the mall parking lot captured the woman. This video and photo had been distributed to the surrounding police agencies. It appeared the girls had gone with her willingly. The parents of the missing girls didn't recognize the woman or her car. The car had been reported stolen yesterday morning.

A patrolman that worked the red-light district had recognized the driver. She worked the streets. She was cleaned up in the mall video, but he was sure it was her. They had picked her up within an hour of the video being distributed.

I was present at the Everett Police Department when 21-year-old Lucy Lowendowski had been brought in for questioning. She claimed she'd been given instructions to befriend young pretty girls and get them to leave with her. She was to drive them to a designated Safeway parking lot and park next to a white van. Her pimp had told her it would be an easy two grand upfront and she wouldn't have to lie on her back for it. He'd said the vehicle was just stolen and hadn't been reported yet and they'd never be able to pin it on her.

Lucy sung like a canary. She hadn't recognized the van or the three guys in the van. Checking the video from the Safeway store hadn't helped. The men used a white utility van and the plates had been stolen just that morning. When they arrested her, she had heroin on her and was laying it all on her pimp. The investigation would be ongoing. Lucy identified the girls from the photos their parents had brought in. She said that was the first time she had done anything like that, but she'd needed money for drugs.

"I can't believe what is happening. This is a rough week for missing girls. With females helping to kidnap these girls, their natural suspicions are reduced." I said to Jeff. "I've been seeing more and more of that. These two have just vanished. Jesus Christ, why can't the parents warn these kids not to get in cars with strangers? We can't trust anyone anymore. Shit."

Despite early efforts to locate the pimp, we suspect he was in the wind. The pimps watch their girls closely and he may have seen the police pick Lucy up for questioning. He's known on the streets as *Knuckles*, since he always has a set of brass knuckles on him. If he's still in the area the APB out on him should bring results. He has been known to move from city to city when the heat was on.

"Now we've got three missing girls and dead ends." Jeff said as we left and headed back to the office before going home for the night.

Chapter Twenty-Four
Becca

The next morning, Keilan and Mandy stood on the other side of the cellar door. Keilan sounded mad. "Get Becca. We need to do the photo shoot and get her picture on *Backpage* because the bids are starting to come in. Make sure you brush all the spiders off her before bringing her in the house." Keilan mumbled something. "We have to move everything up because we may be compromised by Connie's escape."

Mandy unlocked the doors to the root cellar. Light flooded down into the cave-like room sunk into the ground. "Becca, get up here Keilan wants to see you." I pushed myself away from the cold, damp wall and shielded my eyes with my arm and climbed up the stairs.

"Shit, you're a mess." Mandy said. "Mud on your face and your hair is matted. Damn."

"What about Jessica and Tina? Are they coming, too?" I asked.

"No, and they aren't your concern. Here are some blankets for them. They will be coming out in a few hours." Mandy threw a few blankets to me. I covered the two girls that were hanging on to each other. I'm just fourteen, but they look younger holding on to each other and their eyes are so sad and scared.

"Here, cover yourselves and I'll see if they will give you something to eat," I said not knowing what else to say.

I briefly remembered my dream and wished it was true, that the cops were looking for me. Then I remembered the Amber Alert. The cops were looking for me. Maybe the dream was real and an angel had spoken to me in my dream. But I don't think so. Maybe Connie got to safety and told the police. Oh dear God, let Connie be safe.

As we walked into the house, Keilan moved toward us. His stance softened as he looked at me. "Oh honey, I'm so sorry that I had to put you in the cellar. I was just so afraid that Connie would give away where we were and the police would come looking for you. I don't want to lose you. Now go get a shower and we will talk about the wedding when you're all cleaned up and have something in your stomach."

He was so gentle and kind as his hand brushed against my cheek. It's like he is two different people. Maybe everything is going to be alright.

Mandy pointed me to the bathroom. "I will get you some clean clothes. There's a hair dryer and curling or flat iron in the cabinet and makeup in the top drawer."

The chill in the cellar along with my fear left me shaking. I've never been so afraid in my life.

I don't understand what is happening. Keilan isn't angry anymore and said he didn't want to lose me. He still loves me. I just don't understand. What about Jessica and Tina? Is Keilan in love with them, too? Jessica said they were kidnapped out of a Safeway parking lot. Kidnapped! Is Keilan a kidnapper?

I stepped into the bathroom and started the shower as I wanted warm water to help take away the chill from the cellar. I checked that there was soap, but my body started shaking uncontrollably, and I dropped the soap on the floor.

Mandy tapped on the door. "What's going on in there, Becca? I don't hear the water running."

"Nothing, it's running, I just dropped the soap," I responded. I felt the shower and the heat was starting to fog up the mirror. I stripped off my dirty clothes then climbed in. Under the spray of the water, I folded my arms around my body and cried silently as the water flowed over my face.

Dear God help me, I don't know what is happening and I know I shouldn't have run away from home. I thought I was doing the right thing. I thought he really loved me and we were going to get married.

I wet my hair and added the shampoo. As I washed, twigs and dirt trickled down my body; the water turned a deep dirty brown. I then lathered up a body sponge and tried to rub the dirt from my skin as I broke down into more tears.

When I stepped out of the shower, my dirty clothes were gone, replaced by a pair of panties and a see-through teddy. I quickly grabbed for the toilet and puked out what little was left in my stomach. I heaved until I could no longer bring up anything. Then the shaking started again. Not wanting to be naked, I put on the panties and teddy then wrapped the towel around myself. I was embarrassed and felt dirty in the undergarments. The medicine cabinet had a bunch of toothbrushes still in their boxes and some toothpaste. I brushed my teeth and rinsed out my mouth, then sat on the floor hugging my knees to my body.

Mandy walked in and made me work on my hair and makeup.

"Why do I have to wear this teddy? I don't want anyone to see me in this," I said to Mandy.

"Just do as you're told. You will find out soon enough. Now finish up. I don't have time to coddle you." Mandy frowned at me. "Just pretend you are going on a date and fix yourself up pretty," Mandy said as she left the bathroom.

I quickly lifted the toilet lid and dry heaved again as tears ran down my cheeks. I wiped my face and brushed my teeth again and worked on my hair. Silently, I prayed as I used the curling iron.

Oh God, I don't know what is happening. Keep me safe, please please don't let them hurt me. I am so scared.

A few minutes later, there was a pounding on the door. "Becca, are you finished? Come on, baby, you need to get out here. Everyone is waiting." Keilan opened the door and bent down to grab a hold of my arms and gently brought me up.

"What.. wha… what are you going to do to me? Who is waiting?" I stuttered, shaking so bad I couldn't get the words to come out.

"What? You don't like the little teddy? You picked it out," Keilan said with a little smirk. "We're going to have a little bachelorette party just for you. We are going to take pictures and unveil you to the world. He brushed my cheek and inhaled the smell of my clean hair. "Aw, don't worry. No one is going to touch you. You are being prepped for a very special night. We are only going to take some pictures."

Chapter Twenty-Five
<u>Becca</u>

"Come on Becca, your audience awaits. I've arranged this coming out party just for you." Keilan's tone told me I didn't have any options. "If you don't come out on your own, I will just have to carry you. Do you want me to do that?"

"N-N, I don't want to. Pl-ease, don't make me... I d-don't want anyone to-to see me..." I begged, crying and pulling away.

"Oh, baby, the teddy covers up a little bit and pretty soon you won't have that on. We can't really start the party without our guest of honor. The Virgin Becca." Keilan tipped up his beer and downed the rest of the bottle. "Okay, I've tried to do this the nice way, but you're starting to piss me off."

A shiver ran through me at his words. I reached for his arm desperate to change his mind. "I don't want all these people to see me. Please don't make me do this." I pulled on his arm trying to stay in the hall as I could hear the people whispering and talking. I let go and quickly headed back into the bathroom to puke in the toilet. I couldn't stop crying.

Keilan grabbed me up and backhanded me across the cheek and dropped me on the hall floor..."Do you want more?" I lay curled up in a ball. Mandy pushed past Keilan and pulled me up. She reminded Keilan that I couldn't have any marks.

She walked me into the living room where people were sitting on the sofa and chairs. Some were even sitting on the floor. I didn't count them, but there had to be at least twenty. There was a camera sitting on a tripod and a sheet against one wall. Mandy walked me over to the sheet. There was alcohol and drugs in a line on a mirror. I looked at everyone looking at me, and hung my head in shame. All the fight seemed to leave me and I felt so hopeless.

Come on Becca, you don't have any choice. You either do what he wants or he will kill you. Just take a deep breath and wipe your eyes. Your life has changed and if you want to come out of it alive, you need to do what he says now, and try to make a plan to escape later.

I wiped the tears from my face. "W-What do you want me t-to

do?"

The morning was spent with me naked and in various lingerie; a house full of people that were drinking and doing drugs stared at me while making comments about how I should pose and how I was going to give some old man a heart attack. Every time I started crying, they would take a break to add more makeup. I was forced to put on clothes that made me look like a school girl. I begged and pleaded with them to let me go back in the cellar. They had to stop when I started to shake so bad the photographer said the pictures were blurry. Then they had to stop as I began heaving some more. I felt so weak and prayed for unconsciousness so I didn't have to see these people. The shame at being surrounded by strangers made me want to die. My head spun and one of the girls offered me some cocaine. Keilan slapped her and said, "My Bitches don't do drugs. The clients want them drug-free, and that's what they will get."

I wish I was dead. God help me, I don't want to do this. Please.

I tried to pull a sheet that was laying on the floor over me, but Keilan said "It's a little late for that isn't it Becca sweetheart? Everyone has already seen what you have to offer. Soon the world will get to see my sweet Becca." His laugh was so awful.

"You said you loved me?" I whimpered.

"What? What are you mumbling?" he said so everyone could hear.

He was making fun of me and they were all laughing.

Keilan took me aside and started with soothing sweet words, like "It won't be much longer. C'mon baby, do this for me?" Then when I started crying and shaking again, his mood would change. "I fucking hate dealing with young girls. They make me crazy with their whining." Then he called Mandy back into the room. "You deal with her, if I stay in here much longer I'm going to beat the shit out of her and I can't do that. She can't have any marks on her on her first date, you know that. Another fifteen minutes and we should be good." Then he walked out of the room.

Mandy wasn't as mean as Keilan. "Becca, you need to straighten up and do as Keilan says. He may not hit you now, but he will make you pay later."

"Why is he doing this to me? I thought we were getting married and he loved me?"

"God, Becca, how fucking stupid are you? He never loved you. He isn't capable of loving anyone. You're his whore now. He's going to pimp you out. Do you get that?" she said slowly while cupping my chin and staring into my eyes. "The sooner you cooperate, the sooner you can go back to your dungeon."

"But I'm a virgin," I said, crying.

"Yes, you are, that's why Keilan found you so special. Virgins get a higher price, especially if they're under the age of 15. Actually, the younger the better. These pervs pay a special price to be the first."

"Our sweet little Becca is going to make some lucky guy very happy soon. Just wait until they get a load of that sweet body that has never been touched. They will pay lots of money to be the first, a virgin; they will pay a lot of money to do that bitch." Keilan got cruder and repetitive the more alcohol he drank. He smelled sour whenever he came close to me.

Why didn't I see him for the way he really was? He isn't the Keilan that talked to me on the internet or that was so gentle and kind when he picked us up at the airport. Connie had seen that in him, but I wouldn't listen to her.

"This bitch is going to make me lots and lots of money, aren't you, Becca baby? Your pictures are being uploaded now. The bidding has really started to get serious. You were worth every penny it took to get you here Becca baby, but I will just add that to what you owe me for all the nice things I bought you at the mall, you and that Connie bitch." Then he got angry again. He seemed to enjoy being the center of attention. "If I ever see that bitch again, they won't be able to find her bones, I promise you that."

"Enough about that bitch, I want to be happy. Have you got enough pictures?" He asked the guy taking the pictures. He nodded. "Then take the bitch back to the cellar." Keilan pointed to Mandy. "Get her into some jeans and a sweater so she doesn't freeze to death before her big day." He laughed as I walked back to the bedroom with Mandy.

The cellar sounded nice compared to being in front of all those people without any clothes on. Oh, dear God, are they going to do this to Jessica and Tina?

I heard Keilan explaining to his crowd how furious he was when the Amber Alert came out. He would have beaten me then, but he said he had to wait until he sold my virginity. The pictures were uploaded to a live feed and within a few minutes, he said the bidding closed at $6000 for 6 hours with me. $1000 an hour, Keilan said the buyer could do whatever he wanted short of crippling or maiming me. I had to be left intact so Keilan could still sell me again and again. He had advertised me as a tender, young girl with soft, velvety skin. He said once he sold me as a virgin, he wouldn't get that price again. In his words "I would be soiled goods."

Mandy gave me some jeans and a sweater and took me back to the root cellar. She took Jessica and Tina and said it was their turn.

Chapter Twenty-Six
<u>Becca - Rape</u>

I lay in the corner of the dingy motel room. The shaking wouldn't stop. My body felt broken and dirty. I had no more tears, unsure how long I'd been in the dark. How long the stranger had been gone. The wall heater ran, but I couldn't get warm. I couldn't move. It hurts to move. I reached up and pulled the blanket off the bed and wrapped it around me.

No one is going to find me and no one is going to want me. I felt his hands on me. Don't touch me, I remember screaming, but no one comes. He covered my mouth with his big hands and I tried to bite him, but he backhanded me and told me if I screamed again, he could kill me and no one would care. Keilan sold me to him and he could do anything he wanted to me. He was going to be sure and get his money's worth, even if it killed me. He smelled of cigarettes and some kind of aftershave or cologne that made me want to puke. He was breathing his hot breath on me and I prayed to die. Keilan made me dress up like a Catholic school girl in a plaid skirt white blouse and sweater, knee socks and tennis shoes. Mandy put barrettes in my hair and told me I needed to act like an eleven-year- old. I want to go home. Oh God, what have I done? I want to die.

These thoughts raced through my mind as I cried myself to sleep beneath the blanket. It couldn't have been for very long. I heard the card in the door and prayed that he wasn't coming back. I tried to move even farther into the corner, farther into the wall, but I couldn't hide.

Make me invisible, don't let him see me.

Mandy turned on the light and walked into the room then shut the door. She walked over to me and soothingly said, "Come on, Becca, you have to get up. The worst is over now. Come on, you can take a bath and wash up." Mandy got me to look at her. She motioned over to the baby monitor sitting next to the bed, then put her finger to her lips in a shushing motion for me not to say anything as we were being monitored. She took me into the bathroom and started running a hot bath for me. She gave me the soap, knowing I'd want a lot of soap. But no matter how much soap she gave me, she said it wouldn't be enough.

While the water ran, Mandy whispered in my ear "The worst is over now. Things will never be good, but they will be better than this. Pretty soon you will be numb. Just don't make Keilan angry. You are his property now, and he won't let you forget it." Mandy tried to pull the blanket from me so she could get me in the tub. I held on tightly and refused to let it go. A softness in Mandy and her gentle cooing eventually persuaded me to let it go and get in the tub. Mandy said, "I'll be outside in the room and will give you some privacy. Don't take too long, we don't want to keep Keilan waiting."

Clean, I can't get clean. He said he loved me. I'm not a virgin anymore. My body hurts so badly. My arms are bruised and my legs are bruised. I can't get clean, not enough soap. Not enough soap. Why me, dear God, why me? I want to go home. I want to go home.

I cried as the warm running water rained on my head.

Mandy brought my clothes into the bathroom and helped me get dressed. She said that Keilan had left and the monitor was gone. Then we walked out to the car. I felt like I was in a fog and I had to hold onto Mandy to keep my legs from buckling under me. I just want to go to sleep and never wake up.

Chapter Twenty-Seven
<u>Skye - Nunnehi</u>

On the flight back from North Carolina, I slept and had a dream about Becca. I saw Becca led by a dark-haired woman to a car parked in a lot that had a flashing sign that said, "No Vacancy" below a sign that said, "Capri Motel." Becca wore a red and black plaid skirt and a white blouse. She moved slowly and held onto the woman for support.

At first, I wasn't sure that it was Becca I saw; there was something different about her hair. The sky was getting dark and there appeared to be heavy cloud cover so the colors weren't very good. Then I saw a close-up of the girl's face and I recognized Becca. I also saw the woman's face. She had dark brown hair and looked about 25-years-old.

They got into an older Jeep but there wasn't a license plate, or it was obscured.

A bell dinged and Grammie shook me awake. "Skye, we're landing, so you need to buckle up. We should be there in about ten minutes."

"Okay, I was having a dream about Becca. At least it felt like a dream." I looked out the window and noticed the sky darkening like a storm was coming. The sky looked the same as in my dream. Maybe I was seeing Becca in real time. "Grammie, I need to call Detective Alex as soon as possible. Do you have her number?"

She patted my hand and tried to calm me, "Well, we're landing so we can't turn our cell phones on. We will call her when we get off the plane"

Grammie handed me Alex's card. I was twisting my purse handle and I began fidgeting. I wanted the plane to land and it seemed like it was taking forever. As the seat belt sign went off, I jumped up and was cutting in front of people and tried not to be rude. I told Grammie, I'd wait for her in the concourse.

As soon as I got in the concourse area, I dialed Alex's office. "Detective Prosser, this is Skye Frost."

"What can I do for you, Skye?" She sounded distracted. It sounded like she put her hand over the phone and was talking to someone. "I'm sorry Skye what were you saying?"

"I know this is going to sound crazy, but is there a Capri Motel around Lynnwood?"

"Um hum, I'm not sure…"

The detective started to answer when a loud speaker in the background came on. "The plane to Los Angeles is now boarding at Gate 3D. The flight to Los Angeles is now boarding at Gate 3D."

"Where are you Skye?" she asked.

"I'm at the airport."

"Oh, okay. What were you saying about the Capri Motel?"

"Is there such a place in the Seattle area?" I asked. *Come on say there is, please say there is.* I was biting my lip.

"I believe there is. Why is that important? Just a minute, let me think."

With the pause in the phone, I felt anxious, like time was slipping away. "I think Becca may be there in a Jeep," I said. "I will explain later, but I think you should check there. Please hurry, it looked like she was leaving in a Jeep." The phone slipped out of my hand and when I went to pick it up, we were disconnected.

***

Alex

I was not at all comfortable with going on a wild goose chase, but what did I have to lose? Nick was chasing another lead so I grabbed one of the other detectives and said, "Sanchez, do you feel like going for a ride? I just got a tip that one of our missing girls may be at the Capri Motel. Do you know where that is?"

"On Broadway. It's a dive motel, if that's the one you mean?" Sanchez gave me a questioning glance.

"Let's go, I don't know, we'll see."

Sanchez and I arrived at the Capri Motel. There were no cars parked in the lot, so we headed to the office. The dark-skinned middle-eastern man at the counter looked up at us as we walked into the lobby. His eyes went immediately to my badge on my belt.

"How can I help you detectives?" he asked with a strong accent.

I showed him my badge and pulled out a copy of a photo of Becca. "Have you seen this girl?"

He looked at the photo and shook his head. "No. No one like that."

"Your sign says, 'No Vacancy.' Are you full?"

He scowled and turned and said something to a young man sitting in the next room. "Ah, no detectives, just the opposite. We don't have any customers. My son switched on the 'No Vacancy' sign by mistake."

"Well have you had any guests in the last half hour? Where is your sign-in register?"

He handed me a printout and I read a scrawled signature. The make and model of a Jeep Commando and an Oregon license number were listed.

"How long ago did this vehicle leave?"

"About twenty minutes ago. They paid in cash. The woman registered last night."

"Detective Sanchez, get as much information as you can from Mr. Ahmed Borkez. I need to make a call." I stepped outside the door and ordered a search warrant for the Capri Motel and requested a patrol unit to escort Mr. Borkez down to the station for an interview. I also ran the plate listed for the Jeep which belonged to a Ford Taurus. The plate had been reported stolen a week ago. Then I put out an *all points bulletin* on the Jeep, last seen with two female occupants.

"Damn, we may have just missed Becca by twenty minutes. Where in the hell are the Frosts getting this information? Something smells fishy about this whole thing," I mumbled under my breath.

The search warrant garnered a lot of cash, far more than could be made from a second rate motel. Though, it's hard to prove that the funds were illegal. Hard to prove they were funds from human trafficking. The interview was unsuccessful in getting anymore leads, but the motel was now on the watch list. Since we didn't have proof that it was a human trafficking case, but only classified as a runaway, our forensic resources were limited.

ANN KIDWELL

Chapter Twenty-Eight
<u>Becca</u>

The day after I was raped, Keilan beat me with his fists and a belt. But not where it would show. He grabbed my hair and paraded me around in front of his friends naked. I prayed that he would just kill me and get it over with.

Mandy told Keilan, "If you keep beating them, you are just beating up your investment. You took the time getting Becca, and killing her isn't going to benefit you."

I'd heard him tell Mandy one time when she tried to get between me and him. "You know how this works, rape and beatings let them know that they belong to me and I can do anything I want to them." He never raped us, but would let a friend rape us while he watched.

The shame and degradation left me hollow inside. I was sick from being punched in the stomach and had a hard time keeping food down.

How can anyone treat another person like this? I don't want to live anymore. I want to go home and see my mother and my sister. Thinking of them is the only thing that gets me through. I keep having dreams, when I finally get to sleep, of the Indian girl and her telling me to hold on, that the police are looking for me.

Keilan now kept me, Jessica, and Tina in a locked room of the cabin with a surveillance camera on us. Our every move was monitored. We were locked in and had to knock on the door or talk into a surveillance camera to get someone to let us out to go to the bathroom or bathe. At least it was warm and dry.

Later in the second week, Keilan had me get in the front seat of his new Lexus. "You're going for your branding, bitch." I didn't know what that meant, but Keilan said I would find out soon enough. I figured it was a tattoo like Jessica and Tina had, but I was hoping it wasn't that. I didn't want to be labeled someone's property. I noticed earlier in the week when Keilan was hitting me, that he no longer had the tattoo of "Rebecca" on his arm. *That must have been as fake as he was.*

Keilan drove for about 10 minutes then pulled out onto a dirt road. I was forced to wear sunglasses that were made like a blindfold and I couldn't see anything. Mandy was beside me and admonished me to not take them off or try to see outside of them, as that would garner me another beating. Keilan had waited a while after my rape, until the bruises had faded, before he took me to the tattoo artist. Even though the tattoo artist called *Pig*, knew Keilan trafficked in young girls, he didn't want to elicit any sympathy from *Pig*, that the bruises might bring. He told Mandy, *Pig* already knew too much. He had done tattoos for Keilan before and he knew what he wanted. It was a tattoo of a spider web on the upper left thigh, about two inches square, and Property of Weaver, below it. This let others know that I was Weaver's property.

I'd been sullen and quiet since the rape. I didn't want to be seen or heard. Keilan said, "That's good, keep your mouth shut, Bitch, I don't want to hear your whining anyway. Get over it." That was his key phrase along with, "It's done and can't be undone." He always said. Mandy had been a little protective of me. She had tried to keep me out of his sight except when necessary, like today.

Once the tattoo was done, he could start putting me to work and earning my keep. That was the way he put it.

"Jessica and Tina have both been bringing in cash. They weren't virgins, but they cleaned up nice and weren't near the trouble as this Bitch," Keilan said, slapping the back of my head.

"Damn, I hate virgins," he said out loud.

I shivered, sitting next to him. *To think I was in love with him. Mom was right; I wasn't old enough to know what I was doing. If I could just undo what I have done. I see him differently now. He is the most evil person I ever met.* A tear rolled down my face. I was a captive, and I had no say on anything that was or would be done to me. Keilan elbowed me out of my thoughts.

"You will get your tattoo and not make a fuss, do you hear me?" he whispered in a tone that warned me not to cross him.

I uttered a sullen, "Yes" without looking at him. I hadn't said much to anyone for the last week. I would just go in and out of a fog brought on by the beatings, little to eat, and all the retching. I'd been doing. I had been bathing a couple times a day and just laid curled up on a mattress on the floor, listless.

No one will ever find me. No one will ever come to save me.

The tattoo parlor was a dingy backroom with a shop out front. *Pig*, as he was called, was big and sweaty with a bandana on his head. He looked like a dirty biker. Wearing a vest, his large stomach pressed against me as he talked directly to me. He smelled of weed and sweat.

"Pull your jeans down. Come on, I'm not going to hurt you. Pig doesn't hurt little girls. I like mine with more meat on their bones, so I'm just going to put a little tattoo on your thigh."

I broke away from him and ran for the door. "No, no, no! Don't touch me! I won't do it again. No, I want to go home. Don't touch me!" I screamed at the top of my lungs.

Keilan grabbed me in a bear hug and told Mandy to get the tape and put it over my mouth. Mandy did as she was told and my hands were soon tied behind my back.

"Haha, you got a firecracker there, Keilan. Let's get this done. Still want the web with a spider in it and property of Weaver?"

Keilan nodded yes. "That's what the boss wants."

"How many girls you got running now?" Pig asks.

"Not enough. These bitches cost money and this one hasn't yet earned her keep."

After the tattoo, Keilan took me to a doctor, a client of Keilan's, to get me checked out. He had an agreement with the doctor that he gets to give all Keilan's young girls a checkup and gets to be the first to sample them, except the virgins.

Mandy had told me about him. "He had an office in the back of his home. You will be subjected to an invasive physical exam and then raped by him. So be ready. In return, the doctor will insert a birth control implant in your arm so there is no chance of any unwanted pregnancies. He said your periods are less and that means less down time. That way Keilan can keep you girls working and doesn't have to deal with cramps and that PMS shit. Also, if one of you gets an STD, the doctor will take care of that. He calls it the Weaver Benefit Package."

I was sore from the tattoo, but the doctor did just like Mandy had said. He seemed to take pleasure in his examination of me. He wasn't gentle and he didn't say a word except when he told me to hold still or to roll over. It was sterile with no emotions. He smelled like rubbing alcohol and mediciny. I just closed my eyes and tried not to look at his face. When he finished examining me and raping me, he put the implant in my arm. Then he walked out of the room without a word and sent Mandy in. I couldn't cry anymore. I was just numb.

Chapter Twenty-Nine
Becca

The tattoo hurt and was red but Keilan said I just needed to "get over it." We moved from the cabin into a house closer to the city. He told me we would be going back and forth. I wasn't' sure what "close to the city" meant. I didn't know what city we were near, Keilan kept us locked in a room all the time. The windows had bars and were frosted so we couldn't see out. It let in a little light, but we never got to see out except when leaving the house to go to the car. All of the time he made us wear those glasses. He had a camera set in the corner of the room and someone watched us at all times. I know, because when I tried to get out or tried to open the window, someone showed up at the door and told me to sit back down and stay away from the window. I talked to the camera or banged on the door to let them know when I needed to go to the bathroom. Someone would let me out, but I would be watched. Keilan told me and the other girls, "It beats the cellar. If you try to escape, it's back to the pit."

We were driven back to the cabin. It only took about twenty minutes. There didn't seem to be any houses close to this house either. They didn't appear to have neighbors as I listened for traffic or any other noises that might indicate there were others around. Hoping that if we could get away and walk to a nearby house, business, or someplace where they could call home or the police.

There was no furniture in the room, just a pillow in the corner. Sometimes an old mattress was in the room and a couple of blankets. For one brief second, I managed to slide the window open and I thought I saw a large white bird land on the branch of a pine tree just outside the window, like before. But they told me to close the window and get away from it, so I wasn't sure.

Jessica and Tina were shoved into the room by Keilan. "If you bitches want to eat, you better behave yourselves. You brought in $300 between the both of you today. That's not enough. You will have to do better tonight. It's about time for Becca to earn her keep. Enough coddling Becca, you've got some dates lined up for tomorrow. Jessica, you and Tina fill her in on what's expected."

Jessica was dressed in a tight short skirt with four-inch heels and a cropped top hanging off one shoulder. Her hair was teased and sprayed and she wore deep red lipstick and mascara. The makeup looked trashy. Tina was similarly dressed. I hadn't really seen either one of them much since being in the cellar. When they'd come in late at night I was sleeping or pretending to be. I just wanted to go to sleep and never wake up.

"What did he make you do?" I asked each of them.

Jessica answered, as Tina stuck close beside her and still didn't appear to want to talk.

"He sets up dates over the internet and Mandy takes us to an old dirty motel and walks us to the room. She tells us what the customer wants us to do and we do it. She collects the money and waits in the room next door. She listens on a baby monitor and would know if we asked to use their phone or tried to call out on the room phone. Then we would get another customer and another and another. We didn't have much time to think about the next one. Sometimes the customer would want both of us at the same time." I reached over to lay a hand on Jessica to comfort her. Her eyes filled with tears. "We tried to resist at first, but every time I said, 'No, I'm not doing that,' Keilan would punch Tina in the stomach. We learned quickly that we didn't have a choice."

Jessica took a deep breath and continued. "The first time Keilan took us to the motel, I tried to open the door and jump out and run when we got to the motel, but they wouldn't open. Keilan laughed and said he had all the doors on his vehicles equipped so that the doors could only be opened with the key fob. We were trapped every time we got into the cars."

My heart broke and we all cried and held on to each other. I feared for what would become of me and them.

Jessica continued through a broken voice, "We feel so dirty and can't get the smell off of either of us. I'm so afraid for Tina. I don't know how she can keep going. She hardly speaks or sleeps, and wakes in the middle of the night screaming. She has never been very strong. Do you think our parents are looking for us? Do you think they will find us?"

Jessica's questions burned in my heart because I didn't know how anyone would ever find us.

"I'm sure they are looking for both of you. Someone will find us… I hope. I don't know about me because my family's in Detroit and that's a long ways away. I ran away with another girl and we flew here to meet Keilan. I thought he was my boyfriend, but he just pretended so he could sell me," I whispered to Jessica.

Jessica listened then asked with a horror-stricken face, "Where's the other girl? He didn't kill her, did he?"

"No, she got away and I hope she's safe and tells someone where I am. That's my only hope. She tried to get me to go with her but I thought I was in love with Keilan and he felt the same. I was so stupid. I should have listened to her. She said it just didn't feel right."

I began work the next day. If that's what you want to call it. I was still sore from the repeated rape from my first. I will never forget his filth and his smell. With Keilan's beatings, the first rape, the tattoos and the doctor, my whole body was tender and sore.

Keilan and Mandy set up dates on the dark web and on *Backpage*. Mandy had five men scheduled. "Johns" she called them. If they had bought girls from Keilan before, Mandy knew how they liked it and would instruct me on what to do. She said five was what she had set up for each day this week, then the count would go up.

She would collect the money and get feedback from them on how we did. She would report any bad feedback to Keilan and he would beat us again in front of the others to make a point.

I was younger than the other two but more combative and drew Keilan's wrath if he was pissed about something. I knew that Tina was in a fragile state, so I tried to draw him away from her when he was mad. We all had to work now. I was numb and like the other two, just trying to survive. It had been about two weeks as far as I could remember. Each day ran into the other, and we were losing hope of being found. We had no phones or TV to measure time. We were completely isolated except when we were working, if that is what you want to call it. When I wasn't in a hotel room, I was asleep trying to escape through my dreams.

ANN KIDWELL

Chapter Thirty
Skye - Nunnehi

I'd returned with Grammie to my home in Lynnwood. She flew to her home in Eastern Washington. It was hard for me to let her go. When I was a little girl, I always cried when she left. Today wasn't much different. Tears welled up in my eyes. It felt like she was taking my heart with her.

I was no longer afraid of my shadow, but I was hesitant to reveal what I went through in North Carolina, because Grammie said not everyone would believe me. I needed to keep my Cherokee name a secret at this time and only share it when I must. The night we got back from North Carolina, I stayed up late telling Papa some details about the naming ceremony and my Animal Spirit Guide.

"We are in a battle to save the lives of those who are living in hopelessness and as these crimes against children are in the shadows, we must fight in the shadows," Grammie had told me. "There is a movement to bring this out of the shadows but that will take time and we don't need to reveal our hand."

The next morning, I called Detective Alexandra Prosser, to make an appointment to share additional information. She said she was getting ready to call me about the Capri Motel but said she would talk to me when I got to her office.

Later that afternoon, I was directed back to Alex's office. "Hi, Skye, how are you? You look different. I can't put my finger on it, but did you get some sun in North Carolina?"

"Maybe, a little."

"Anyway, the trip must have agreed with you. You look radiant and absolutely glowing."

"Thank you. Yes, I learned a lot and met my Great Grandmother, Takena, on the Cherokee Reservation."

"The last time I saw you, you didn't mention that you were going to North Carolina. Is everything all right with your family?"

"Oh, yes. My Grammie had to get back home to Grandpa so she left last night."

"Yes, I was surprised when you called. I expected to see her with you, since I know you are very shy and feel more comfortable with her beside you."

"Detecti... I mean Alex; yes I am shy, but I am working on that." I said still feeling nervous. "I came here because I need to explain some things to you."

"Okay, Skye, why don't you have a seat and we can talk." Alex pulled out a chair for me to sit in.

"I went with my Grammie and my cousin Aaron to the reservation where she grew up. We went there because she said I needed to get in touch with my heritage." I took a deep breath, feeling nervous but continued. "She said that I was exhibiting a gift that some Cherokees exhibit in their teen years, the gift of sight."

Alex appeared to consider what I'd just said. "What do you mean the gift of sight? I'm a person with an open mind, but I don't buy into the psychic stuff," she said."

"Remember when Grammie called and told you the part about the rest stop and that the girls were there? That was what I saw in a dream. The one girl, the blond one, was trying to escape and she was hiding in the bushes while Mandy and Connie looked for her."

Alex looked at her watch and said, "Let's pause here. It is past lunch time now. How about I buy you some lunch?"

"All right," I said and we left the office.

"I know this nice restaurant just across the street. You get a good lunch at a price a detective can afford."

"Yes, that sounds good." I said.

After we ordered and got our drinks, the conversation continued.

"I can't get over how much you've changed in just five days. You exude a confidence now that is different than when you were here last week." *Even the shade of her eyes seems to have changed with flecks of gold.* Alex thinks.

"Are you telling me that you saw this in a vision? That you're psychic?" Alex asked as she finished her burger.

"No, I'm not psychic, but I do have an animal spirit guide, sometimes called a totem, that lends me his eyes to see through."

"Well, I wasn't ready for that answer. I don't understand," Alex said with a puzzled look on her face.

"It's a long story" I pushed my plate to the edge of the table. "While visiting my Great Grandmother, I had a vision quest and found out I was born with a Cherokee gift. She said that it usually becomes apparent in the teen years." I took a deep breath. "Grammie, was the one that noticed it when I told her about Becca and Connie."

"Told her what about Becca and Connie?" Alex pressed.

"That I saw Becca up close when the plane she flew from Detroit to Seattle was circling the airport in a holding pattern before landing and that was what drew my attention to her. Remember, you asked me what it was that got my attention about the girls?"

"Yes, I remember. Go on."

"It's hard to explain and I'm afraid I'm muddling this all up. But the snowy owl comes to me in my dreams and many times when I'm awake. I didn't know what was happening when I first saw the girls at the airport. I actually saw Becca **before** the plane landed. While they were at least a half-mile away in the sky. I just shrugged it off as my imagination. And no, I don't do drugs, any drugs," I said.

Alex's eyebrows arched in a look of disbelief.

"I want to help but I need to keep my gift a secret. Most people don't believe in such things. I can tell you don't believe me either. My Great Grandmother said this gift was given to me for a reason and I must not squander it." Taking another deep breath, I sat back in my seat.

I continued "My Cherokee name is Nunnehi, spelled N u n n e h i. Which means *Graceful Warrior* and in other translations, "*The little one or the invisible little one.*"

The look on Alex's face said: *Is this girl crazy?*

"I can tell from your look that you don't believe a thing I've said."

"Well, I admit I'm having a hard time swallowing this. I just don't know what to say?" Alex shrugged her shoulders. "Go on, I want to see where this is going."

"Okay, I'm still learning how to use my gift. I'm able to speak to Becca through her dreams to let her know she is not alone, but she can't speak to me and it almost always happens in her dreams. I don't think she recognizes them as anything more than dreams, right now, but I hope she will catch on soon. I will try to get a message to her or try to send some clue through Casper's eyes. That's what I call my spirit guide, *Casper* because he appears ghostly white to me. I'm still honing this gift. It has only been a couple of days and I don't really know the scope of what I will be able to see in the future. But I'm hoping to help save Becca. I just don't know how to explain it any better." I let out another deep breath, and watched Alex's face. She dabbed at her mouth with her napkin and cleared her throat.

"Wow. I don't know what I expected. I don't even know where to go with this."

She thinks I'm crazy. How can I convince her? What can I do to show her?

"When I got off the plane last night, I called you and told you about the Capri Motel."

"Yes?"

"Was that a lead? I know you can't tell me about the case, but did it help at all?"

"No, I can't really discuss the case with you, but it was something we checked out."

"This has changed me. All I ever wanted was to lead a normal life and enjoy my senior year and my dancing. I'm on the dance team at school and that's my passion. But my priorities are different now. I can't quit thinking about Becca and Connie, and I feel helpless because I can't give you more."

"Speaking of Connie, we found her and she is home now with her mother. Connie told me what happened at the rest stop. How she got away. It all fit with the call I received from your Grandmother from North Carolina."

"Really?" I couldn't help it, I cried.

"We are still searching for Becca." Alex said.

I hesitated and swallowed hard. "I'm sorry for crying."

"The fact that Connie said she was at the rest stop is one of the many things that are forcing me to at least believe some of what you are telling me. The rest stop; the owl; Connie mentioned Becca saw an owl outside of the house she was in. Those all point toward what you've been telling me."

"Connie is okay." I said. I couldn't quit smiling. "So maybe you believe me a little bit?"

"Well, let's just say I will check out your story about North Carolina. You understand I have to do that?"

I nodded my head.

"But if you want, you can call me if you get anymore dreams or visions from Casper, or whatever. For now, okay?"

"Okay." I agreed. "Can we keep Casper our secret for now? It's hard enough in high school; I don't want them to think I'm a loon?"

"Yeah, your secret is safe with me, for now."

"Maybe someday people will recognize that just because they don't understand something, doesn't mean it isn't so." I said.

***

Alex

She's asking me to believe in something that I can neither see, nor verify. I need tangible proof, hocus pocus won't get me a search warrant. I'm at a loss. What I can't figure out is, how would she have this information, otherwise? I can't just take this on blind faith alone. Wow, my head is spinning. I was not prepared for this.

"You're a brave girl to offer help and I will protect your secret as much as I can." With this, Skye nodded. "Here is my cell number and I will list you as a CI. That means confidential informant. Though it's going to be hard to explain how you know these things, I trust you, and we will work around that. Call me anytime, day or night, if '*your eyes in the sky*' show you anything. Also, just refer to me as Alex unless you are calling the police department, and I will call you Skye. How's that? I will use Nunnehi as your *CI* name. Is that alright with you?"

Skye nodded yes. "I just hope I can be helpful. It is overwhelming that Becca's life and being found may hinge on me learning about my gift and how to use it."

While we sat finishing our lunch, I shared with her some of the details that didn't compromise the ongoing investigation. I told her how Connie escaped and explained what I believed had happened to Becca.

"Becca and Connie were lured to Seattle after Becca and Keilan, (not sure if that is his real name or not) chatted online through social media like *SnapChat*. Keilan led her to believe that he was twenty-one-years–old, came from a well-to-do family and was in business with his father. He told her that he couldn't help himself that he had fallen in love with her. According to Connie, he said all the right things. Connie said Becca had problems in school and her mother was placing more restrictions on her because of her grades. She believed everything that Keilan had told her. He convinced her to run away. Becca was naïve and innocent. Becca convinced Connie to go along."

"Yeah, I heard that in the bathroom at the airport," Skye said.

"Do you know what human trafficking is?"

Skye nodded her head yes. "Yeah, we heard about it in school. One of our competing schools did a dance routine about human trafficking but I never knew it was happening in the United States."

"Unfortunately, that is what a lot of people think—it happens elsewhere and not here. It does happen in our own backyard. Girls may be recruited by people they know at school. They may coerce them by holding something over them or threatening to do harm to their family. They are made to feel they have no other options but to do what the trafficker wants."

"Another method is what Keilan did. The trafficker shows them a lot of attention and makes them think they are in love with them. Then the trafficker asks them to do things that are unfathomable to them because they are supposed to be in love with them. It's a contradiction in trust that sends all kinds of warning bells. They think that this part is only temporary and it will get back to the way it was."

I could see the shock on Skye's face.

"Now I understand more of what Casper told me in my Vision Quest. This is the war I need to help fight."

I went on to explain to Skye, "The law is changing in how they treat children that were formerly arrested for prostitution. But the victims think they will get in trouble for being a prostitute, and the trafficker uses that scare tactic to keep them from getting help."

"You mean they don't get in trouble for being a prostitute?" Skye asked, looking puzzled.

"No. Many of the laws have changed and they are seen as victims. A child is not viewed as a willing participant in sexual acts. Traffickers are facing enhanced punishments and longer prison sentences. Men are not the only ones that traffic in children or young adults. Women are also being charged with trafficking in an alarming number of arrests. With women luring young girls, their guard isn't up as much. The victims tend to feel safe with a woman.

Trafficking has been going on for decades and through technology, it has become a multibillion dollar enterprise. It has moved from the streets and gone out of the public's view through the dark web or internet publications like *Backpage or Craig's List*."

Not sure how much I should divulge to Skye, I felt safe with what I had told her.

Skye shook her head. "This is happening in Seattle?"

Yes, Skye, "girls are being abducted in malls as young as eleven. Gangs are selling young children into prostitution because they are seen as an unlimited renewable resource."

I wish I could tell her we have been tracking a group that we think may have Becca. This group lures young girls and boys through elaborate social media contacts and gets them to meet them. They transport them out of their known area. We think we know the name of the person that is the head of the organization. He has his victims tattooed **Property of Weaver** *below a spider web on the left upper thigh. Local and national agencies have joined forces in trying to break up this ring of predators.*

***

Skye

I was relieved that Alex believed me but this new information has pulled me into an ugly and dirty world. I already feel changed from my vision quest. I had been oblivious to what was going on around me I no longer feel safe and now I share in the fear and terror that Becca must feel. Anger coursed through me. I will do whatever I can to save Becca and others like her.

All I was interested in was enjoying my senior year. These victims don't get to have a senior year. I hope God will help me make a difference.

I pulled a note out of my purse and handed it to Alex. "Just before going to North Carolina, the morning after I saw the girls at the airport, I woke from a dream and wrote it down. In the dream I saw Becca and Connie looking out a window of a ranch-style home. Becca was pointing at something and smiling. I'm not sure if it will help, but it might."

Alex reviewed the note and said "Connie talked about that morning. She said Becca saw a large white owl in a tree. Connie thought the information about the owl would help us find their location. She also told us about a house which sounds like the one in your dream. What are these numbers here?" Alex points to the note.

"Oh, those were on the mailbox at the house. Maybe it's an address. Is that helpful?"

"Oh, I could hug you. It may just give us a place to start. Thank you. Call me if you have any more dreams, and please stay safe," Alex said as we left the restaurant.

We headed back across the street to the police department where I left my car parked. "Thanks Alex for believing me." I said as I got into my car. I really felt more relaxed now that I told Alex about my gift.

Chapter Thirty-One
<u>Alex</u>

I dropped Skye at the mall and headed back to the office to track down the latest lead.

I called a meeting of the task force and shared the information about the number and had them check with all the surrounding area 911 centers to see if they had any houses with that sequence of numbers. Maybe this is the lead that will take us to Becca. The adrenaline coursed through my body. A silent prayer was whispered though my lips. "Please, God, give us a break in this case."

It didn't take long for them to locate the house described in Skye's dream.

My team and I headed to the house with a search warrant and hoped they would still be there. I know from experience the traffickers don't stay in one place very long. Since Connie got away, they may have left that place, but it's a lead. I'm determined to save at least one girl.

Our team arrived, but it looked quiet. The house was a rental so we tracked down the owner and went by his house first to find out who his tenants were. He said that they were good renters and had been there about three months. They paid a large deposit and three month's rent in advance. He hadn't received any complaints from the neighbors and said it didn't get much better than that. The owner was home alone so I left a copy of the search warrant and an officer with him. He gave us a key and said, "Please don't break in the door like they do on television."

No vehicles were parked in the drive. We knocked and when no one answered we used the key to let ourselves in. A copy of the warrant was left in the house. When we got inside, we found that it was stark and appeared to be a transitional house that they could leave quickly. There were dishes on the table, no pictures on the walls, a dusty spot where a television may have sat. There were just the barest necessities like toilet paper and some old towels. There was milk and some beer in the refrigerator but that was it. We were too late. But they had been there, which meant we might get some fingerprints or other leads from the house.

Unless we get some identifying prints, I've hit the wall again. He's good at hiding. *Your time is coming, you bastard.*

ANN KIDWELL

Chapter Thirty-Two
Becca

I saw a calendar in one of the sleazy motels and it had the date of September 27. That means I have been here almost three months. Only three months. It feels like I have been here for years. I don't remember what normal is anymore. Every day is the same, just different men, but the same outcome. We're all exhausted and usually fall asleep as soon as our heads hit the filthy mattresses on the floor. Jessica is getting an attitude and Tina is getting weaker. She barely eats anything. I don't know how much more we can take.

We were moving from the cabin to the other house in no particular pattern that I could figure out. Jessica, Tina and I were violated day after day and night after night. I heard Keilan tell Mandy they couldn't use the Capri Motel anymore as it was being watched.

The cabin was deep in the forest and had no close neighbors as far as I could tell. Only a few cars go by each hour. The chance of someone accidently finding us was remote. *I've got to escape. I've got to get away or I will die here and my mother will never know what happened to me.*

Jessica, Tina and, I had been allowed out more lately. Keilan said our color wasn't good and the customers don't like sick-looking whores. He got a large pit-bull to scare anyone that might come around. He named the dog Duke and said he was for protection.

Keilan told us he likes everything neat and tidy because he has an image to maintain. He assigned us the job of cleaning up the yard after the dog. At least we are out of the house for a little while. Even cleaning up dog poop is better than being in the room and worrying about what comes next.

The nightmares never end. An endless number of men in all shapes and sizes crawl all over me and I can't get the images out of my mind. I can't escape the stench and can't wash it off. Jessica and Tina feel the same way.

We were out in the yard with Mandy who was reading a magazine and talking on her phone. I tossed the ball for Duke and devised a plan to try to slip away and find someone with a phone we could use. I thought we might have a chance of getting away.

While outside, I saw a large white bird circling the house. It looked like the one I saw in my dreams. In my last dream, I followed the bird and ran through the woods. There were wild blackberry bushes scratching at my arms and face but I was getting away in the dream. Now that I saw the bird again, I thought it might be a sign that now would be a good time to try to escape.

"Jessica, throw the ball to me and I will throw it to Duke. You are such a good boy, Duke." I said as I bent over to pet the large dog. Duke stayed close to Tina, drawn to her for some reason. Maybe he sensed her vulnerability. He had to be persuaded to leave her side but he liked running after the ball.

I whispered "NOW" and pointed out a trail. They agreed and quietly headed down the path. Mandy's back was to us. She was laughing and talking on the phone.

We were gone for about fifteen minutes before we heard Mandy and Keilan yelling for us. We stayed off the path. We heard a car every now and then. We were afraid to go to the road because Keilan would more than likely drive down the road. We needed to stay under the cover of the forest. It was getting dark and the temperature was dropping fast. Tina lost steam and fell behind when we came upon an old garage with old unusable gas pumps. The light was on in the office part. I tapped on the window and a young guy came to the door and seemed surprised to see us out there.

"Where'd you all come from?" he asked.

"Just back in the woods. We got separated from our family and have been trying to find them. Can we use your phone?" I asked.

The young man saw the dog and asked, "He's a big dog, does he bite?"

"Only if you try to hurt Tina. He protects her. Can we use your phone?"

"Sure, I'll go in the back and get it."

I looked up and saw the white bird sitting on a branch of one of the tall pines, but then it flew away.

The young man came out from the back, just as the silver Lexus pulled up.

Keilan got out of the car and walked over to the young man. "Thanks, Ben. Here's a little something for your trouble." We grabbed each other's hands and squeezed ourselves into a huddle.

"I wouldn't have known they were yours except for Duke," Ben said.

Keilan opened the back of the car and told Jessica and Tina to get in and lie on the floor like they are supposed to. Keilan looked at me and grabbed me by the hair. "You're responsible for this, aren't you?" I tried to pull away from him but he threw me toward the back door of the Lexus. I knew that when we got back he would beat us.

"I don't care anymore and I will keep trying until I get away from you – you bastard!" I screamed at Keilan.

Back at the house, Keilan told us to get ready because we had already missed one appointment and we would have to make that up. He said, "Your punishment will wait 'till we get back. Money, first."

Chapter Thirty-Three
Skye-Nunnehi

I was listening to my music while doing my homework when my vision changed. I looked down from high above the trees and then the scene below became clearer. I took the earbuds out of my ears and closed my eyes to focus my whole attention on what was unfolding. In my mind's eye, it was much like looking through a telephoto lens. Though my view was from high in the sky, I could see the rustling of underbrush in a dense forest, very similar to the surrounding Cascade Mountains but I wasn't sure of the exact location. In my vision, Casper also focused on a winding road from the aerial view which appeared to be two to three miles from any of the main highways. My vision sharpened on the road. I made out three individuals and a large dog appearing to be headed toward that road. They were running, but not on any established trail. My vision stabilized. Casper must have sat on a branch. I recognized Becca as one of the three even though I noticed her hair was shorter and dyed red. She was in the lead with the other two following. They are young girls, maybe 14 or 15 years old. Becca looked right at me with recognition. *Recognition… recognition of Casper, the owl. She remembers seeing Casper. Becca now has a connection with Casper, and through Casper, to me.*

A gas station came into view just ahead of where they were going. I hoped they would continue in that direction and possibly find some help. Casper took flight again getting closer to the garage. The building was nondescript - no markings, and there were no street signs to help me pinpoint their location. I am still learning to communicate with Casper through my thoughts. He flies a little closer but there are no distinguishing features, except that it sits at a curve in the road and has a single island of gas pumps with out-of-order signs on them.

Becca stopped with the girls as they huddled in the brush and looked back the way they came. They looked scared as if someone was following them. Casper left his perch and flew past the girls in the direction they came from. I could see Keilan and a dark-haired girl, the one I saw at the motel, appearing to be searching for the girls. I could tell they were yelling. I prayed that they could get help at the garage before Keilan could find them.

The three figures and dog stayed off the path. The light was getting dimmer as the sun was setting and I could see the smallest girl shivering and crying. She was dragging her feet and leaning heavily on the dog when they came upon the old garage.

Casper flew back to perch on the branch where there was a clear view of the garage. The light was on in the office part and Becca tapped on the window. A young guy came to the door and seemed surprised to see them out there.

She was talking to him and made a motion of putting a phone to her ear. He looked behind her and focused on the dog and the other two girls. It appeared he was going to pet the dog but backed away instead. Becca again made the motion of talking on the phone. The guy closed the door and disappeared from the garage window.

Becca shuffled nervously and kicked at the ground while rubbing her hands together. She looked up at me. No not me, but Casper. She was focused on Casper. She had recognition in her eyes. She was putting it together.

The young man came out from the back just as the silver Lexus pulled into the garage area. Keilan got out of the car and walked over to the young man and shook his hand. I saw him pass Keilan some money. The guy pointed to the dog and appeared to call the dog to him.

The girls grabbed each other's hands and pulled themselves into a protective huddle. The scowl on Keilan's face was sheer anger.

I could read Becca's face as she screamed, "No…no…no…no!" A deep despair settled over me as I watched helplessly. The girls held each other and he separated them and sent the two girls to the back of the car, then grabbed Becca by the hair and shoved her toward the car.

He put Becca and the dog in the front seat and then he got in and drove away. Casper's vision went to the license plate, but something obscured the plate. Then my mind's eye went black.

I crumbled to the floor and pounded my fists into the carpet, all the while sobbing and screaming, "No… no, dear God no, no, no, no."

Papa rushed into my room and grabbed me and rocked me as I cried and babbled into his chest.

"Skye, oh, Skye, come on, baby, don't cry, please don't cry. Everything will work out. Shush, it will be alright," he cooed as he continued to rock me back and forth. He mumbled, "This sight is not a gift, but a curse."

"Papa, I felt so helpless." Grabbing his shirt and crying into his chest. "I couldn't do anything; nothing, just watch it happen. I don't know if I am strong enough to do this." I couldn't stop shaking, just uncontrolled shaking. Like that little girl. "Papa, he has three girls and they were so scared, I could feel their fear."

Papa hummed some unknown lullaby from when I was young. Papa continued to rock me until I let go of his shirt and looked up to him. "Papa, I have to call Alex and tell her what I know. What little I saw. The silver Lexus, but I couldn't see the license plate. I hope she can get something from that. It just happened so fast. Oh Papa, I wish I could have done something."

I had calmed enough to make the call. He hugged me and said he felt helpless to help me because he doesn't have any of the "Cherokee Gifts." Then he stepped out of the room.

I explained to Alex what I had witnessed. I told her about the garage and Keilan coming and getting them. I told her about the young girl and she said she would bring some photos by to see if I could identify them.

"I'm so sorry you had to witness that, Nunnehi. Try to get some rest and I will stop by in an hour or so. In the meantime, I am going to see if we can get a location of that garage with the description you gave me."

Papa stepped back into the room about fifteen minutes later and pulled a blanket over me and kissed me on the forehead. He hugged me to him.

When Grammie and I had returned from North Carolina, Papa had said he knew that I had gone through a change, and Grammie had told him what the changes were. She'd explained I had witnessed a case of "human trafficking" at the airport. She had filled him in on everything.

"I don't like the idea of you witnessing things like this. I'm worried about you. These are dangerous people. I know you have this power, but it doesn't make you infallible."

"I know, Papa, but I can't turn my back on this. I have to help the only way I know how, with the strength of my gift."

"Oh, Skye, honey, I love you, and I'm here for you anytime you feel overwhelmed." He pulled me to him and I sobbed some more. "I had no idea human trafficking happened in the US, let alone in our own neighborhood."

"Oh, Dear God, keep Skye and those girls safe," he prayed.

Chapter Thirty-Four
<u>Alex</u>

It had been three months since Becca had gone missing when Nunnehi called me and told me that she had seen Becca, two other girls, and a dog trying to escape in the forest. She couldn't get a street name or location, just that she had seen a gas station on the curve of a small road and the gas pumps looked too old to work. She had also seen Keilan driving a new, silver Lexus but the license plate had been obscured. It wasn't much, but it was something. There were two other girls with Becca. And the dog was protective of the smallest of the girls. Becca's hair was now short and red.

I called the task force together and had someone from the GPS department assist us in locating garages on curves. I also had people checking on owners of a new silver-colored Lexus. It was a long shot, but we had to work with what we had.

"We need to get photos of any recent missing girls with blond hair, taking in consideration that their hair may be dyed also. My CI (confidential informant) saw two young blond girls with Becca. They appeared to be 13 or 14. My source may be able to identify the girls with Becca if we can get a photo montage together."

Photos on a zip drive in hand, I headed to Skye's home. When speaking to her on the phone she had sounded like she had been crying. I couldn't conceive what seeing those things must be doing to her. I had told her I would come by her house in an hour or so and show her some photos of missing girls matching the descriptions she had given me.

Ryan answered the door and led me to her room. It was a typical teenage girl's room with fairy lights and mirrors. She had pairs of dance slippers hanging on one wall along with ballet related paintings which were treasures from her Grammie.

I pulled out my tablet and inserted the thumb drive that had photos downloaded of the areas missing girls. Within a half hour she had picked out Jessica and Tina.

Skye started crying again over the fact that the girls had looked so scared. Her whole body shook. I couldn't help but hug her and let her know that her help was a blessing in letting us know they were still alive.

This was terribly hard for her, and it made me question the toll this was taking on her. "Sweetie, I'm worried about how this is affecting you. It's hard for me and I'm trained to deal with this stuff."

"I'll be okay. I was given this gift for a reason which means I must be strong enough to handle it. I can't stop now, even if I could, I wouldn't. I need to help you find Becca."

Chapter Thirty-Five
Becca

It was October and I had been gone for over three months. It seemed like a lifetime. After the attempted escape we were no longer allowed outside. I had overheard a lot about what Keilan was doing in addition to selling us.

I learned, listening to various phone conversations between Keilan and Mandy with a man named Mason, that in addition to us, they had four high school girls turning tricks. They were all from different schools so they couldn't get together and talk. It was Mandy's job to get them to their appointments after school. They could each work three guys a night. They were able to keep them in line because they each had younger sisters or brothers that he threatened to kidnap if they didn't go along with it. One of them was tweaking on drugs and he warned her if she was caught again, her baby sister was going to take her place. These girls were from foster families and they ply the foster parents with excuses for going out or coming home late.

Keilan had told Mandy they were expendable and there were many more where they came from.

These girls were easier to manage since he didn't have to keep them locked up or have to worry about kidnapping them. He used intimidation and threats to keep them in line. Three of the four had been working for him for more than a year. He had one close call when one of the girls challenged him by threatening to go to the authorities. After he locked her away for forty-eight hours in the dark, damp root cellar, she'd had a change of heart. All he had to do was show the other girls' pictures of her when he took her out. That was enough to scare the other three, but he was going to have to move along. He didn't like staying in one place too long and risk being discovered. When he left, he would just sell them to a pimp in the area. They were in the business now and were going to stay in the business as long as they could bring in the dollars.

Keilan had praised Mandy for doing a good job of managing them. She said she had known what he expected and she got it done. From these conversations, I also learned Keilan no longer made her service "Johns" as long as she managed the other girls when he needed her to. Besides, she was over 21 and most "Johns" liked them younger. He provided Mandy with coke and she got to keep the proceeds of one of the girls. The girls got nothing. They were allowed to go home at night and keep their siblings safe.

Chapter Thirty-Six
__Becca__

I escaped into my dreams each night after I had been molested by more men than I could count. Exhausted, I usually fell asleep after scrubbing my body raw with soap in the shower. That is where I did my crying, too. I tried to put up a strong front for Jessica and Tina, but I didn't feel it. Every hour of every day I felt hopeless, praying that someone would find me, or that I won't wake up in the morning. I would welcome death over this.

Tina is getting thinner and thinner and I'm afraid if she doesn't continue to work, Keilan may decide to get rid of her. It enters my mind that we could be killed at any time and left to rot in the forest. I set aside some of my food hoping Tina will eat it and get stronger. She appears to have lost the will to live. Jessica tried to pick up the slack, but she has heard Keilan talking to Mandy, that if she can't continue to perform, he will get rid of her. He talked about giving her to another pimp to handle but I told him that Jessica and I would pick up the slack and so far, that has worked.

By the time my head hits the pillow each night I'm so tired, but I have been having very lucid dreams. I wondered if Keilan is putting something in our food. What I thought was an Indian girl with white wings became clearer and had morphed into a Native American girl with a large white owl. She had long black hair braided and a band on her forehead with beads and feathers. Her eyes are a beautiful deep brown with gold flecks. A buckskin dress with fringe along the bottom and beads around the neck and shoulders completed her native dress. Something else I noticed was that she had a leather shield wrapped around her left forearm and on that sat the large white owl. The dreams are so real and the girl seems familiar, but I don't know from where. The owl was the same as the one I had been seeing flying overhead lately. I thought it was the same one that I had seen that first morning out the window of the first house we had been in, at the rest area, and when we were escaping. For some reason, just seeing the big white bird gave me a glimmer of hope, but only briefly. My tendency toward despair overwhelmed me again.

I want to die. I'm a coward or I would find something to help me end this pain. The beatings or the threats of beatings don't scare me anymore. Maybe if he hits me just so, that will end it for me. It isn't just the act of so many men violating me repeatedly and having no regard for what it's doing to me, it is I have no say in the matter. No escape.

151

My space, they are in my space and I have no escape. I try to escape in my mind and in my thoughts but they won't even allow that. I am so tired.

I am made to participate in those vile acts. I am flesh, blood and bone. I had dreams and wishes and plans. Now I have nothing.

I think of my mother and Sissy and my dog. I will never see them again. Has Mom given up hope on me? Has she stopped looking for me?

How much longer can I last? Will they just throw my body in a dumpster when the life has left me? Will the things I have done keep me from going to heaven? I'm so tired.

Please I beg you, let me escape into my dreams. I have no will, no strength, no thoughts, no space, no soul. I am but a shell, a vessel for another to use. I am so tired.

The person I was has ceased to exist. In her place is a numb girl going through the motions just to survive.

I have to keep telling myself to fight and not give up. Don't let the bastards win. Don't let the bastards win. Take back your soul. Don't let the bastards win. Again, I had cried myself to sleep.

In my dream, the Indian girl made a sign with her index finger held to her lips then moved to her ear indicating that she cannot hear me speak. At first, I thought she must be telling me not to tell anyone about my dreams. I tried speaking to the girl in my dream, but she seemed unable to hear or understand me. It's quiet in my dreams except for a low drumming noise in the distance. I am able to see the owl flying in the sky and then return and land on the Indian girl's arm. The Indian girl is surrounded by a forest, but it's different than the Seattle forest. The forest in my dream is like they have in eastern Tennessee where the trees turn all different colors in the Fall. I used to travel there in the summers to visit my relatives.

These dreams are so peaceful and I look forward to them, though they don't come every night. I know that it's probably my imagination. Maybe it's a way for me to cope with what was happening to me. But just the same, it's an escape.

In this dream, I heard the girl speak to me. "Becca, do not despair. The police are looking for you and the other two girls. They know you are in the Cascade Mountains." She also told me, "Connie is safe and the white owl's name is Casper. He is my eyes. I see what he sees. When you see Casper, know that I am also with you." I began to cry. I wanted this dream to be real. Dear God, let this dream be real.

The dream gave me hope and a renewed determination. Those bastards will not win. I will see them in hell first.

Chapter Thirty-Seven
__Becca__

It is now November and Tina had withdrawn more. For the last couple of weeks she had been steadily wasting away. She is dying right before my eyes.

I developed a plan to get Tina help. I worked extra hard pleasing my *Johns* and Tina's *Johns*. After I serviced a *John*, Mandy always asked them how things went and what they could do to make things better. It was Keilan's strategy – his way of getting noticed by his boss, Weaver. I made sure those reports were good. I wanted to make myself indispensable to Keilan, and get more leverage for what I wanted. Things hadn't changed with reference to our living conditions. We were kept in a locked room and monitored constantly. I pretended to be compliant. Keilan made a lot of money on me and he started to feel secure that he had broken me. I couldn't wait any longer; time was running out for Tina.

"I won't do anymore whoring for you - unless you take Tina to a hospital." I threatened. She's curled up in a ball and hasn't spoken for days."

Keilan Just stared at me, with a smirk on his face.

"She's sick, for God's sake!"

I watched his right hand. It was balled into a fist.

"You can beat me or kill me. I don't care if I die, but I won't watch her die."

Keilan just shook his head and glanced over at Tina lying in the corner. The veins in his neck bulged blue and pulsed.

"You know that I am your best girl and I bring in the most money. Tina can't work in her condition. If she dies, it will take weeks to get another girl ready for Super Bowl week."

"Shut the fuck up, or I'll beat the shit out of you!" Now he is seething. His face is red.

I pushed on. "You'll be down two whores on Super Bowl weekend if you beat me up. Johns don't like seeing bruises." I paused a minute to catch my breath. Keilan looked away, thinking.

"Help Tina!" I said. "I'll do her Johns and my own, too, that way you won't lose anything. Just help her!" I had tears in my eyes.

I was desperate. "Plus, I promise I won't try to run away again!"

"I'm supposed to trust a whore?"

"I may be a whore, but I don't lie. Please... Help... Tina!" I begged.

Keilan, calmer now, scratched his head. "Let me think about it. You promise you won't try to run away, again, and you'll pick up Tina's Johns?"

I nodded.

He was quiet for a little bit, then grabbed my arm and said "I wouldn't even consider this if I could get someone ready in time for the Super Bowl. So that's your "ace in the hole" and you better not cross me or you won't make it to a hospital when I'm done with you. Are we clear?"

At the end of the evening, he agreed, but as usual with Keilan, it had to be done his way.

Keilan agreed to have Mandy take Tina to a remote town and call it in. He said not to go to a hospital because there were too many cameras.

Tina refused to go without me sitting in the back seat with her. Mandy took us in her Jeep and drove to a town called Issaquah. The area was remote so we wouldn't be seen.

I helped Tina out of the car to a spot not far from the road and sat her on the grass. I softly spoke to Tina. "Tina, sweetie, I'm going to call an ambulance to come and get you." I kissed her on the forehead. "Please, baby, hang on and fight. Don't let Keilan win."

I turned to run to the car and thought I saw a large white shadow in the trees and heard an owl hoot, but then it was gone. When I got in the car, Mandy gave me a burner phone, and I called 911. I told them where Tina was.

Mandy pulled down the road and when the ambulance arrived she removed the battery in the phone and threw it in the bushes.

Later that night, I was exhausted and dropped to the floor in the corner of our room and said a prayer. I hoped Tina was getting help, and I shared that with Jessica.

***
Alex

As dusk settled in, I received a call from Nunnehi.

"I saw Becca leave the cabin in a Jeep, with the dark-haired girl driving. Then Casper went dark."

"About an hour later Casper sent me images again. He showed me a sign saying "Welcome to Historic Issaquah." The Jeep parked along a road in a wooded area. I saw Becca getting out of the Jeep with a girl that was smaller than her and had straight blond hair. She was holding the girl up. It looked like a park. Becca leaned the girl against a tree. Then she ran back to the car and they left."

"Casper stayed focused on the young girl and in about five minutes an ambulance and police car arrived. I didn't get a license plate on the Jeep. That was all I got. I'm sorry it isn't more."

"That's a lot Nunnehi; we will get right on that." I hung up the phone and *Googled* parks in Issaquah, and then I dialed the Issaquah police department. I was immediately transferred to a detective.

"Detective Woods speaking, how can I help you?"

"Hello, Detective Woods, this is Detective Prosser with the Lynnwood Police Department. We just received information that you picked up a girl in a park a few minutes ago."

"That's my understanding and they have just transported her to Swedish Hospital, but that call just came in. How did you hear about it?"

"I've been working with a CI that led me to believe that girl is a victim in a human trafficking case I'm investigating. I'm on my way there. Would you please let your officers know that I would like to question the girl? I should be there in about an hour. I'll fill you in when I get there. Oh and Detective, would you post an officer there as her life could still be in danger?"

"Will do, see you in an hour."

ANN KIDWELL

Chapter Thirty-Eight
Becca

Life continued but my spirit was numb from having sex with as many as 30 men in a 24-hour period. I tried to make up for Tina as I had told Keilan I would. The person I was just four months ago was gone. I longed to escape but it was useless. Jessica was bitter and didn't seem to care if she made Keilan angry. They both grew accustomed to the beatings. That was how he got his kicks. He liked being in control and inflicting pain.

Keilan didn't like us taking drugs but Jessica had managed to get some cocaine from one of the *Johns*. She said it helped her deal with what she had to do to stay alive. When Keilan found out, he beat her again.

We were shuttled back and forth from the cabin to the house closer to the city. We never knew from one day to the next where we would be. The cabin was nicer and appeared to be something Keilan owned. The house was run down and appeared to be just a transition house.

In the house, we both stayed in a room where we slept on a couple of old mattresses on the floor with a couple of blankets. A video camera was hooked up to a receiver in a remote location so we never knew when we were being monitored. We were fed once a day, if they didn't forget about us. Usually, it was purchased from a fast food place. A place that was open late at night after we were done servicing our *Johns*.

The use of a baby monitor in the motel rooms was a common practice and usually Mandy was in a room next to or adjoining where we met the *Johns*. Jessica had tried to get a *John* to let her use his phone so she could get a message to her mother, but the *Johns* knew not to ever let the girls use their phones. It put them in danger of being arrested so that was a no-brainer. The time that Jessica had tried, she had paid dearly for it afterward.

They upgraded the baby monitors they used to include video that someone could actually watch everything we did. Keilan had said, "Some people really get into that shit. You never know Becca, you may someday be a porn star," and walked away laughing. That had sent chills down my spine and I prayed he wasn't putting those on the internet.

Chapter Thirty-Nine
<u>Alex</u>

I arrived at the hospital in Issaquah unprepared for how frail the young girl in the hospital room looked. She must have only weighed about 70 or 80 pounds. Her features were hollow and her eyes sunken. She wouldn't look at me and stayed curled into a fetal position.

The hospital had brought in a psychiatrist/social worker to assist me in speaking with her, but she had buried her head in the pillow and refused to talk with either of us. The doctor said she had given her a sedative and an IV to provide nourishment. I hoped the girl might feel more like talking in the morning. I gave the doctor my card and asked her to call when the girl woke up. For her safety, I had the Issaquah Police Department keep an officer stationed outside her door.

I checked through the photos Nunnehi had picked out, and she was a hollow shell of the girl in the photo. It was Tina Miller, missing for over four months.

The next morning the doctor called and said that Tina ate a light breakfast and may be willing to talk. When I arrived, I brought a stuffed lion and some daisies for her. My heart just broke when I saw the broken child.

"I've called your mother and she should be here shortly."

Tina cried. "I'm so ashamed and if I tell anyone what I've done, they'll put me in jail. My mother won't love me anymore. I couldn't help Jessica. They have Jessica." She broke into sobs and her whole body shook.

I held her in my arms and let her cry, cooing to her. "You haven't done anything wrong. Shush... shush... little one, you haven't done anything wrong. You have nothing to be ashamed of. I know your mother is worried sick about you and will be happy that you are going home with her."

"I've done some bad things," she cried.

"Hush, baby. Your family loves and misses you and are thankful you're alive. They should be here any time."

I turned to the doctor. "Can we go out in the hall and talk?" The doctor pointed to the hall. Once out of earshot, I asked. "Tell me, doctor, will she be okay? From what she's been through she is lucky to be alive. But I need to ask her some questions, so that we might find her friend Jessica." The doctor said that Tina can talk if she felt like it, but suggested that I wait until her parents arrive.

About that time, a commotion erupted at the nurses' desk. "Oh, dear God, where is my daughter? Is Tina here?"

I put my hand out and introduced myself. "I'm Detective Prosser from the Lynnwood Police Department. If you'll just follow me, I'll take you to your daughter. You need to know that she has been through a lot and needs all the love and kindness you can give. She's afraid you will judge her, so it's important for you to treat her gently. None of this is her fault."

"I'm Sandra and this is my husband Ted, and all we want is our daughter back."

"She's right this way, but she looks very frail so I want to prepare you ahead of time. The doctor says she will mend physically, but this was emotionally very traumatic for her."

The parents acknowledged this. Doctor Meyer introduced herself to the parents and said, "I'm going to let you see your daughter and we can speak afterwards. Just let the nurse know when you're ready and she'll page me."

As they entered Tina's room, even though they had been warned, they were not prepared for the vacant look in their daughter's eyes. Mrs. Miller rushed to her daughter's side and hugged her and kissed her head and face and couldn't quit crying, "You're okay, you're okay, Thank God you're alive. God, I prayed every night you would be okay. We love you and have missed you so much. Everything will be okay. Everything will be okay now." Tears ran down my face as I watched the reunion. I told the nurse that when they were ready to speak to me, I would be in the cafeteria.

Ted and Sandra Miller walked into the cafeteria, grabbed some coffee and sat down with me. "I'm so sorry that this happened to your daughter and your whole family. I can't imagine what you have been going through since Tina and Jessica went missing."

"Where is Jessica? Tina said she is still with *them*. Who is *them*?" Ted asked.

"We're not sure yet. We believe that Tina and Jessica were

kidnapped by a group that traffics in young girls. We have some ideas, but they have been very careful and we are still tracking down some of the leads," Alex explained to them.

"Who is Becca?" Sandra asked.

Alex looked at Sandra and asked, "Did Tina mention Becca?"

"Yes, she said that Becca was the one that took her to the park. Do you know what she is talking about?"

This confirmed for Alex that Nunnehi's information about Becca leaving the girl in the park was correct. This was the lead they were looking for. She needed to speak to Tina as soon as possible. She might have some details that would help them find Becca and put an end to this trafficking ring.

"May I speak with Tina some more? She may have some information to help us save Jessica and the other girl, Becca."

Ted said, "Yes, but the doctor just gave her another sedative to help her sleep. We want to help anyway we can. Jessica is like a daughter to us also."

My phone vibrated. "Excuse me, I have a call I have to answer." Another girl had gone missing a few nights ago and she had been linked to a conversation with a Keilan on social media. She was a foster child that had run away a couple of times so it was overlooked until the social media connection came through and explained the sergeant on the other end of the phone. "I'll be in the office in about an hour so get me everything you have on this one."

Tina was sleeping now so I gave the Miller's my card and told them to call when Tina woke up and I would come back.

ANN KIDWELL

Chapter Forty
Alex

Based on the information I had received from the social media posts and the text history off the missing girl's phone, I believed Keilan had lured another girl into his trap. Foster children are easy prey. Trafficking rescue organizations refer to foster children as "high risk for trafficking." Many times they are not monitored closely and many exhibit rebellious attitudes. She had been texting Keilan, talking about getting out of this latest foster home. She was unhappy and felt the foster parents just used her as a slave to do their cleaning. This information was obtained from her cell provider. The recipient's phone had gone quiet and untraceable.

She was 14-years-old and had lip and eyebrow piercings. Her hair was shaved on one side and bright orange on the other. She had a tattoo of a dove on her shoulder and a Keebler Elf on her tummy. Her choice of fashion was a mid-thigh pencil skirt with tights, ankle boots, and a sweatshirt with the hood cut off.

She was last seen climbing into a silver Lexus.

***

Becca

I awoke to the door opening and Keilan shoving a very angry young girl into the room. Her hands were duct taped behind her back and she kicked at him and tried to scream.

"Becca, you can take the tape off of her after I get the door locked. You bitch, you're lucky I didn't break your neck for biting me. You thought you were like a slave to your foster parents. You're going to learn what being a real slave will be like," Keilan chuckled as he slammed the door.

Jessica and I worked together to take the tape off her and tried to settle her down. "What the fuck is this place and who are you?"

"Be quiet or he'll come back in here and we'll all pay. Sit down and we'll tell you what's happening. What's your name?"

"Penny."

After I told her what was happening, Penny leaned back against the wall. "Nobody is selling my ass. It's not going to happen." She sounded much braver than I'm sure she felt.

I tried to calm her down, but I knew the fear she was feeling. I also knew how futile being angry was. I pulled her over to the corner, away from the camera and whispered, "Penny, are you a virgin?"

Penny hung her head. "Why are you asking me that?"

I told her what was done to me, and what she could expect.

"I know I don't look it, but I am."

"Does Keilan know that you're a virgin? Have you told him?"

"No, it never came up. I think he just assumed I wasn't, because all we talked about was my getting out of the latest foster home and partying. I act tough to throw people off, so I don't get attacked by my mother's boyfriends or the creepy foster dads." Penny started to cry.

"I don't know how much they can hear, but if you don't want them to know, you need to turn your back to the camera and whisper. I don't think they are recording it, just monitoring when they feel like it," I said. "I'll turn the light out because then they can't see us talking and I don't think they can hear us when we whisper."

In a whisper, Penny shared her story. "I'm in foster care because my mother is on meth. I smoked cigarettes to look cool, but I don't really like them. I've never done drugs and was too afraid to after seeing what they did to my mom. She would do anybody and anything for her next fix. I have a baby brother who is in the system. I was hoping to find him someday. He's about two now."

She sighed. "Some of my mother's boyfriends tried to make nice with me, if you get my drift. That's how I got in the system, because I broke the last one's nose. I thought by making myself ugly, no one would bother me. I guess there's always one. Keilan thinks he can make money on this skank, but who's going to want to do me?" Penny grabbed my arm and told me she was scared. "Nobody will look for me. Foster parents don't care where you are as long as the checks come in on time. If I ever get out of this, I want to find my little brother." Taking a breath and wiping the tears from her eyes, she said, "If I work real hard, I can probably clean up real good and maybe someday find my baby brother and get custody of him." I wiped a tear from my eye and tried to be strong for Penny.

The girl drew in a deep breath and asked me, "The first time, does it hurt? What do I need to do to keep from getting STD's? What about getting pregnant? I don't want to get pregnant."

I continued to whisper. "The first time it does hurt, but only for a few minutes. You feel it physically, but the feeling of having no control on what someone can do to you hurts much more. It's different with each *John*. Some get off on the fight, others are turned off by that, so you never know what is going to set them off. I try to close my eyes and pretend I'm somewhere else. It works some of the time, but not most."

I was tired but I wanted to put Penny at ease. "Keilan controls everything about us. He makes sure a baby isn't in the mix. He says his whores don't need to look like drugged up hookers. We aren't high price Hollywood escorts, but we are better than the average street hooker, in his eyes. He has Mandy get us all the female items we need. He calls it his "health benefit package" for his girls. Just don't make him mad because he just wants an excuse to hurt you. He gets his kicks by hurting people."

"Yeah, I get that," Penny said. "Who's Mandy?"

"Mandy does Keilan's bidding. She takes us to our "appointments" most of the time. She interacts with the *Johns* collecting the money and watches and listens on the baby monitors that are in each motel room to make sure we are doing what we are supposed to. She also checks with the *Johns* to see if they were happy with our service. It's sick and depraved, but Keilan insists that she do that." I continued, "Mandy does the shopping and gets our "necessaries" like our monthly stuff and takes us to the doctor to get a birth control Implant. Keilan said whores are bad enough but he doesn't want to risk us getting pregnant. He has a doctor on his payroll. The doctor keeps us disease free. He takes what he wants from us as payment. That's the deal," I explained to her.

The next day would be a long one for Penny. Keilan no longer tried to be nice. As a matter of fact, he preferred to have a reason to hurt her.

"Try not to give him any reasons," I warned her. When we rolled over to go to sleep, I could hear her crying for what seemed like hours until I fell asleep.

ANN KIDWELL

Chapter Forty-One

Becca

Penny is taken to Pig for her branding tattoo, then to the doctor for the implanted birth control. The doctor said he would get payment later as he had just been called to the hospital.

Keilan took us to a sleazy motel where he had some *Johns* lined up. He had four rooms in one corner of the motel. A room apiece and the room he watched and listened to us being raped by what seemed like an unlimited number of men. We are only 14 and 15-years-old, but feel so much older, when we take the time to feel anything at all. I'm sure that I will just die someday and no one will miss me. Jessica had turned hard and no longer cared about what happened to her. But she told me she said a prayer each night for Tina.

We watched as Penny was forced into a room where she started to beg, "Please don't make me do this. Please? I will do anything else, but don't let strangers rape me."

Her tears made Keilan smile. "Where is the tough little bitch that bit me last night? Now you get yours. I made it a point to get crazy Hal for you. He likes it rough so you are in for a really good time."

I knew that Keilan had something planned for Penny because he had brought us instead of having Mandy do it.

I hoped Penny remembered about the baby monitors, and knowing that Keilan would be watching and listening to her being raped. I also hoped she remembered, *If they get off on anger and fighting, try to do the opposite and not let her temper get away from her.*

I talked Keilan into letting me go in and comfort Penny after crazy Hal left. Penny was curled up in a ball inside the bathroom. Her bruised and busted lip swelled. I held her while she sobbed in my arms. I helped Penny in the shower and handed her the soap. I noticed a telephone number on the wrapper of the soap to call for help if someone was being trafficked. I took the wrapper and shoved it in my shoe.

If I could ever get my hands on a phone I would call, but I still didn't know where I was because Keilan made sure we wore blindfold glasses and he never parked where we could see signs. Though I see the motel names like the *Capri* or the *Days Inn* or *Super 8 Motel*, I have no idea where they are.

One of these days, he will slip up.

Listening to Penny sob, I climbed in the shower with her and took the shampoo and washed her hair. Then I took a washcloth and soaped it up and slowly washed over the bruises and tried to soothe her. "It will be alright, just let it all out." My heart broke for her.

"I feel so dirty. I begged him not to hurt me anymore and fought, and I scratched him. He just laughed and hit me again. Then I remembered what you said about fighting. So I just cried silently to myself and tried to think of an angel holding me in her arms. When I quit fighting he wasn't happy. He said it was like hitting a dead piece of meat. He was no longer enjoying himself."

Chapter Forty-Two
Nunnehi

I am seeing through Casper's eyes as he sits in a tree looking at the cabin where Keilan is relaxed on the front porch. Keilan had a cup of coffee on a table and was reading a newspaper. All of a sudden, he jumped up and tipped the table over with what must have been a loud crashing. He brushed at his shoulder and neck.

Mandy raced out of the cabin. Keilan had retreated against the wall, still brushing at every part of his body. It looked like he was having a seizure. Though I couldn't hear what was said, I guessed he was screeching, "Get it off, get it off now. Now!"

Mandy looked all around, but didn't seem to see anything. She shrugged her shoulders. Three girls hurry through the sliding glass door and onto the porch. One had toast in her hand. They just stared at Keilan and Mandy. Becca was one of the girls and there was a new girl with orange hair.

Finally, Mandy stomps on the deck then goes over to Keilan, and appears to be telling him, "I got it." I can't read what else she was saying. She was yelling at the girls and shooing them back into the cabin. As she bent down to comfort Keilan, they all ran inside.

The girls watched through the sliding glass door. Keilan finally came out of the spasm he was having.

The porch was a mess, but Casper's sight honed in on the newspaper lying on the deck and I could see *Super Bowl 50* circled on the paper.

Super Bowl 50
Date: Feb. 7th 2016
Levi's Stadium
San Francisco, CA

I was afraid that Becca was dead. It had been two long months since I had had any sightings from Casper until today when I saw the girls. There wasn't a day that went by that I hadn't prayed for Casper to come to me and show me something.

I contacted Alex and told her about the cabin and about the

newspaper with the Super Bowl ad circled.

Alex told me, "The Super Bowl is a big event for traffickers. The intelligence that we have been given is that many of the traffickers are going to be there. We are looking at motel and hotel bookings for that event and trying to get ahead of that operation. The traffickers are getting smarter and setting up private residences and utilizing them as Super Bowl Parties where they can sell their wares to out-of-towners that see ads on *Backpage* or *Craig's List*. We are getting some leads and working on getting people inside the operation."

Every lead that I had shared with Alex had been too late. When they had gotten to the rest area, they had been gone. They had missed them at the motel by 20 minutes. And the house, were already abandoned. I kept racking my brain to find out if there was some way I could get the information in enough time to catch them.

I don't have any power other than what and when my animal spirit guide, Casper, lets me see. He is with me always. I can speak with him and he tells me to be patient, that he has not been able to find them. He spends many nights flying around the cabin, but has revealed no substantial landmarks to locate the whereabouts of the cabin. The car isn't in plain sight so it must be in a garage. I told Alex that it appears to be in the upper Cascades because there is deep snow covering much of the upper elevations right now and Casper has shown me this. I have to just be patient and pay attention to my schoolwork, which I've neglected. Failing my senior year isn't an option and getting low grades isn't either if I want to keep dancing. The girls voted me captain of the dance team which just floored me. It's such an honor but my mind has been on this darker world. How I wish I had never heard of human trafficking. It's a dark and seedy world of oppression and I can't un-know it.

I buried my head in my pillow and cried with frustration and depression as I felt helpless to find Becca. Casper had told me, "Nunnehi, this is not of your making, and though you have this gift of sight, it has its limitations. Becca still needs your help, or I would not be still drawn to the cabin. With that, you need not give up hope." These words of comfort from Casper helped me to keep going.

***

Becca

Keilan came in from the porch and grabbed his car keys. I overheard him tell Mandy, "I'm getting away from here. I'm going into town. Get the bitches ready and I will take them tonight. When I get back, I want you to head to the mall and buy them some clothes for the Super

Bowl and get their stuff ready. I want to leave early day after tomorrow. I'm counting on you to keep our high school girls working. Two more packages are being delivered after we leave. They are young I got them from another pimp. They have only been working for a couple of weeks so they are really green." With that being said, Keilan disappeared down the drive.

Mandy stood on the porch watching him leave then headed back into the house. I asked, "What was that all about?"

Mandy said, "Oh, it was just a spider. Keilan is deathly afraid of spiders. Now, go get ready, Keilan will be back in a few minutes and you'll have to be ready to go to your appointments."

ANN KIDWELL

Chapter Forty-Three
Becca

Keilan had been making preparations for our trip to California for the Super Bowl. He said we were almost ready and others in the Weaver organization were bringing their best girls and they would be making a fortune. It's his opportunity to shine in the organization. He had heard that Weaver himself would be there. He had yet to meet him but had gotten good feedback that he was on Weaver's radar. He had noticed the money and quality of his girls.

He had been grooming us just for this occasion. I heard him telling Mandy that Weaver had a Tudor style mansion in Los Gatos where they would hold the big Super Bowl week-long party. He said he had seen pictures of the six million dollar estate. He hoped to make an impression on Mr. Weaver. Getting as high up as possible in this organization meant more money and power. He would be managing pimps and they would manage the whores. Everything he had worked so hard for was coming together.

Right now, he was just running us three girls but he had been getting us polished up to be "young-high-class call-girls." That's where the money was. He had left Mandy in charge of training to get us there.

"All of this work is going to pay off. They are ready for the Super Bowl party." Keilan said as he praised Mandy.

***

Nunnehi

Two mornings after seeing Keilan on the porch with the Super Bowl ad, I was at dance practice before school. All of a sudden, I saw a mailbox along a road. In the vision it is almost covered in snow, but the wind had uncovered some numbers. I quickly asked one of the girls to give me a pen and I wrote the numbers down. Casper flew around the cabin and that was all I could see. I was back at dance class.

I excused myself and quickly called Alex.

"Thank you, Nunnehi, I will call my team together and see what we can make of the numbers. They were associated with the cabin?"

"I think so. The cabin was in the background."

I'm apprehensive that Becca may be on her way to San Francisco and out of reach for the police to find her. The Super Bowl weekend had always been a fun time I had with my parents, cheering on our favorite team. Knowing the human trafficking aspect of it has jaded how I feel about it now.

I got a vision from Casper about an hour later. I excused myself from the table and headed to the girls' bathroom.

Casper showed me the Lexus pulling out of the drive with Becca in the front seat. I didn't get a good look at the passengers in the car but I think it was Keilan in the driver's seat and two people in the back seat. They were going around some curves and Casper lost sight of the car.

Casper is back at the cabin and focused on another car pulling out of the drive and heading in the opposite direction. A dark-haired girl was driving this vehicle. It's an older Jeep and navigates the snowy roads better than the Lexus. The vision hones in on the license plate and it's clear. It's a Washington plate on a Jeep Commando. I quickly write the license number down.

This is another lead that gives a license plate number. I pray it isn't another stolen plate. I texted Alex the make and model of the car and the plate number and let her know that a girl with dark brown hair was the one driving, the same girl I had seen at the rest area and at the Capri Motel. Alex had told me previously, a dark-haired girl named Mandy worked with Keilan. Now I just had to wait. Casper had gone dark again.

I headed back to my next class but it was hard to concentrate on my instructor. Math isn't my favorite class but I knew I had to pass it to be eligible for the college I wanted to attend.

After school, I called Alex to see if the plate was any help.

"We ran the plate and it came back to a silver Jeep Commando. We are on our way out to the address on the registration. It's in the Cascades so it may be a good lead. I'll call you later and let you know if we have Becca, because I know how much this means to you. Cross your fingers and say a prayer," Alex said.

I waited patiently, but I hadn't heard back from Alex. For about an hour I was able to lose myself in a new dance routine we were practicing for the state finals in March. If it wasn't for having my dance to focus on, I'm not sure I would be able to get by. The music and choreography of the dances were all-consuming and that's one of the things I enjoyed. I may have this gift, or curse, as I sometimes called it, but being a high school senior is what I needed to focus on. That's some of the sage advice that Grammie had given me.

On reflection, I had grown a lot in the last six months. The life-changing experience of going to Cherokee, North Carolina and finding out about my gift, was truly amazing.

I guess things happen for a reason, and that was why Grammie came and why I saw Becca in the airport. She said there is no such thing as coincidences; that things have a rhythm or purpose. She said that we come across people throughout life that we are meant to meet, even if we're not aware of it at that moment. That's why she said it was important to treat everyone with respect and kindness and that you will always reap far more than you sow. God, I miss her.

ANN KIDWELL

Chapter Forty-Four
<u>Keilan</u>

We have Weaver's mansion in Los Gatos during the week leading up to the Super Bowl. We will get there in plenty of time to set up and get my ads on "Backpage" and contacts for the week. Most of the customers during the Super Bowl are out of town people looking to score and make it a memorable week. Money isn't a problem for those people and I can make a killing. With Mandy taking care of things here, everything is going as planned.

Mandy is at the cabin so she can handle the school girls, plus the last two packages that are scheduled to arrive at the cabin. That should keep the money coming in and keep her busy and out of trouble. It's all coming together. It's taken awhile, but I'm getting some notice from higher up. I got a call from Mason. Weaver had noticed the increase in revenue and that there hadn't been any slip-ups. Mason said Weaver had made the comment that, "I'm an example to follow. That I run a tight ship and know how to handle my bitches."

Talk about stroking my ego - that really did. It's made me willing to work harder and do whatever I needed to go up the ranks.

I had told the girls we were going to San Francisco for the Super Bowl. They know they are going to spend a few days on the road where they would get some time off which they were excited about.

The couple of days off will let them rest and freshen up for the Super Bowl Parties. They will be in the car most of the time and they can't get out, unless I let them. Besides, they have settled into a routine now. Plus, I told them I had a surprise for them if they behave themselves. They complained they never get to do anything fun, locked up in that room all the time. I promised them a big screen TV with cable. Becca had asked for some books so I may pick her up a book or two, just to keep her happy. Well, as happy as a whore can be, anyway. Ha!

ANN KIDWELL

Chapter Forty-Five
Nunnehi

Alex contacted me late in the evening just before she went home for the night. I was doing some homework. Alex said that they were still following the lead on the plate.

The plates were for a Jeep Commando, but another Jeep Commando. By the time they had caught up with the owner, they hadn't had the car out of their garage in a few months. Their license plate was missing and they weren't even aware of it until Alex had contacted them.

Alex questioned the owners of the Jeep and found that it had been repaired at a local garage on one of the back roads. They gave her the name and location. It sounded like the one that Casper had showed me when the girls were getting away. They will be checking that out tomorrow morning when the roads open again. It's snowing and the pass is closed.

I was getting sleepy and hungry so I went to the kitchen to get something sweet to eat. My favorite was ice cream. The quart container and a spoon was all I needed. Grammie said I'm one of those lucky people that can eat a lot of high-calorie foods and not gain an ounce. She said she figured dance had a lot to do with that. She liked to do the same thing and she said someday I needed to teach her to dance, before she got too fat!

With the homework completed and my belly full, I plugged my phone into my charger and closed my eyes.

Toward morning, I saw Casper in a dream. I'm aware that I'm still sleeping and continued to open my sleepy mind to what Casper is relaying. We are no longer in the snowy hills of the Cascades but along a highway. It's a large highway and I'm seeing it from high in the sky. I can see a tiny speck that I think is the Lexus. I'm hoping he will get closer so maybe I can get a landmark or highway sign or maybe a license plate. From the conversation with Alex last night, the plate would probably be stolen. That seemed to be Keilan's pattern.

I recognized the highway as Interstate 5 and the sign in the shape of Oregon. Casper got ahead of the car and sat on one of the signs stretched over the highway. I recognized Becca in the passenger seat of the Lexus as it approached Casper's position. Becca made eye contact with

Casper and I knew that she saw the owl. I'm filled with hope that Casper will reveal more but my vision goes dark again.

I woke and hurried to text Alex the information that they are in Oregon on Interstate 5. I wished I could give more information, like a milepost or exit number, but that wasn't revealed.

About an hour after waking up, I saw a breaking news alert about an arrest of a guy named Ben Montgomery on the charge of theft in connection with stolen license plates, but said he is a person of interest in a human trafficking case. I recognized him as the guy Casper honed in on when the girls ran away. His garage is *Ben's Automotive and Repair.*

I texted Alex that Ben was the one that I had seen at the garage. Alex said that he contacted a lawyer and refused to talk. They are still searching for the Jeep Commando and have been unable to get any farther into the Cascades to try to find a cabin that is in close proximity to the garage. A late winter storm was hindering their search.

Chapter Forty-Six
Mandy

There isn't a strong enough word to describe my feelings for him. I'm just glad that he's gone.

As I watched them leave down the drive, I breathed a sigh of relief. I'm going to enjoy my time away from Keilan. I know what has to be done, and I do it because I know that Keilan has people watching me. He has told me as much.

There's nowhere to hide and no one to help me. I learned that lesson well a long time ago when I tried to get away. He toys with his girls and likes to watch them squirm. Giving them hope that they can escape just to come up at the last minute with an "I gotcha." Like a cat toying with a mouse. He said it helps to break their spirit and once he has, their will to fight and leave is gone. Like a caged animal, they are dependent on him to take care of them.

I had just settled in the warm cabin enjoying my freedom from Keilan. The girls did good today and so I picked up pizza on our way back to the cabin. I wasn't sure I would be able to get back to the cabin, but I went around some of the road closed signs and had chains on the Jeep, so that helped. It made for an enjoyable evening and a restful night. I didn't realize how much stress Keilan brought into my life until he wasn't around.

Waking early, I stoked the fire with a good supply of wood from the wood room. I turned on the TV and settled in to have some breakfast. A breaking news announcement showed Ben from the garage being led to a patrol car. "The authorities are on the lookout for a Jeep Commando." They flashed the license plate number across the screen. The newscaster continued, "It is a suspected vehicle used in a human trafficking case. Ben Montgomery of Ben's Automotive and Repair has been arrested on theft charges and is a person of interest in a human trafficking case."

"Fuck." I needed to get out of the area as soon as possible but I couldn't take the Jeep because there's an APB on it. I always changed the plates every week or two but had thought these would be safe since Ben had said they were from a Commando that was in his garage. Now I had to think of another way. Then I remembered the two girls in the bedroom.

To hell with the girls, they'll be on their own I'm getting the hell out.

I could lay up with some friends. Keilan was on his own I'm not going to tell him. Now was my chance, I hoped, to get free of him. He should be getting close to San Francisco today so he wouldn't know unless some of his contacts called him.

Grabbing a bag and throwing as much of my stuff as I could get into it, I bundled up in my snowsuit and called a friend to meet me at the ski resort. Praying that I would get away, I headed out on the snowmobile.

***

Alex

Within the next two hours, the SWAT team surrounded the cabin that corresponded to the mailbox address Nunnehi had given me. We used thermal-imaging to determine that there were two individuals in one of the bedrooms. Checking the garage, we found the Jeep Commando and snowmobile treads lead away from the area. We didn't knock but rammed the door and quickly cleared the cabin. The bedroom was locked from the outside with a slide bolt. Swat opened it to find two young girls crowded into the corner.

I was the next person in the house and ordered my team to help the girls get some warm clothes. "Everything is going to be okay. We'll have you back home safe and sound in a few hours." I smiled gently at them. "Can I ask you a few questions before we leave?" I got a nod from the one that looked the oldest. "How long ago did the person that was here leave? Do you have any idea?"

The smallest one said, pointing to a Mickey Mouse watch on her wrist, "I looked at my watch and it was a little after six when I heard the snowmobile start up. I was afraid that we were going to be left here to starve. Mandy said this was Keilan's cabin but he went to the Super Bowl and Mandy was supposed to take care of us. Do we get to go home now?" She started to cry. Both girls were scared and shaking. They were so young.

"Yes, you get to go home. But first we'll take you into the police station where we'll call your parents to come and get you. Okay?" They both nodded in agreement.

"Damn," *if the news had just waited a few more hours before broadcasting the arrest of Ben Montgomery, I may have been able to have had the element of surprise and been able to catch at least one of these assholes. From the fresh snowmobile tracks it looks like we just missed Mandy.*

I walked over to the patrol car the girls were in and gave the officer orders to take them straight to the station and get the contact information for their parents. I also said to have someone pick up some breakfast for them. "Would you like that?" I asked the two girls sitting in the back of the car. "Let them have anything they want, okay?" I nodded toward the girls and saw the glimmer of a smile on their faces. Before turning quickly from the car, I patted the arm of the female officer driving, "Let's get them somewhere warm and safe."

One of the SWAT team officers came up to me. "Detective, those girls can't be more than 11 or 12 years old. I hope they haven't been missing long." Wiping a stray tear from his eyes, he said, "I wish more of our assignments ended this way."

"I agree, Sergeant, I agree," I said, walking away.

I had the area cordoned off and ordered the forensic team to go through everything for clues. Neither of those girls were Becca, but I really didn't expect to find Becca here. Nunnehi had said that she was on her way to the Super Bowl.

ANN KIDWELL

Chapter Forty-Seven
Mandy

Oh, how I long to have the last three years back. I thought I was so smart and a woman of the world. I'd been a little stupid in high school, tried some of the vogue drugs at the time. I had been lucky or maybe smart, not trying the meth or heroin. I hadn't needed the problems that come with that shit. But I straightened myself out in my senior year. Started college and was going to go to veterinarian school. Then I met Keilan.

I couldn't believe it when I'd met him in the hall of Edmonds Community College. He was watching me and at first it made me a little uncomfortable, but then he introduced himself. He had been so handsome and treated me special. We had dated in a whirlwind of desire. We were hardly ever apart. Then he took me to meet his mother. She was so sweet and he unashamedly doted on her so much. That was the Keilan I fell in love with.

Three months later, we got an apartment together and I thought all my dreams were coming true. He was so thoughtful and was very romantic and charming.

Unfortunately, that didn't last very long. He came home one evening, down in the dumps and said that he had lost his job and he was going to be late on his mother's mortgage. I had never seen him like that before. His depression had been awful and he said that his mother counted on him to keep her safe. He cried like a baby and I couldn't help. I had been living on student loans and barely scraping by. This went on for three days. Then he asked if I would do one favor for him.

That was when my life changed forever along with how I felt about Keilan. Maybe this was when Keilan changed or maybe he had always been like that and I'd just refused to see it. Some of his friends were throwing a party and he asked if I would dance for them like I danced for him. He said they would pay him enough money to make his mother's mortgage payment and it would only be for this one time.

I was floored that he would ask me to do something like that. I refused, but he spent the next few days sulking and moping and said that he was going to leave and move in with his mother since he couldn't afford all the things that we had. My heart broke because I felt I was letting him down and that I would lose him forever. So, I agreed to do it once.

I'll never forget that night. It's burned in my memory. He gave me some Ecstasy to loosen me up, he said. I had never taken it before. The night was kind of a blur, but unfortunately, I remembered more than I'd wanted to. We drove to a large house along a lake. I never knew they made houses that big and plush. Whoever owned that had to be rolling in the money. When we got there, I had been the only girl and there had to be at least 15-20 guys. The music was loud and the booze and drugs were all over.

Keilan got me a few mixed drinks and between the effects of the alcohol and Ecstasy, my head was spinning. I do remember dancing on a table and the guys cheering me on and grabbing at me. Then I was naked and more were grabbing me. Oh, God, how I wish I could forget the rest, but I never will.

The next morning, I woke up by the pool and Keilan put a blanket around me. He was apologizing for having let everything get so out of control. I was sick to my stomach and ran for the restroom where I threw up until I ended with the dry heaves. Then I looked in the mirror. I had bite marks all over my body and I was bruised over almost every square inch of my breasts and legs.

I was so angry and pissed that I went out and started whaling on Keilan, screaming, "What did they do to me. How could you let this happen to me?" I'll never forget the look on his face. He was devoid of any feelings and said, "Boy, baby, did you put on a show. They certainly got their money's worth." He smirked and said, "Your talent would be wasted on veterinary school."

I had screamed and beat on him when he backhanded me and said, "Come on, baby, you just need to get over it." That was his catch line. "You just need to get over it." When I hear those words, I want to puke.

The more I cried, the angrier I got, and the more I hurt inside. Not so much physically, but mentally, I was broken. This just didn't fit and I couldn't believe what he had let happen.

Finally, I told him what he had done was criminal and that I was going to the police. I even told him I was going to go to his mother and tell her what kind of son she had. I hadn't seen the fist that hit me, but I'd been conscious of being beaten about the face and body. I thought he was going to kill me. He would slap me awake and begin again. It felt like it had gone on for hours.

The next day, I woke up in our apartment.

He came into the bedroom like nothing had happened with a breakfast tray with eggs, bacon, toast, and juice. A rose in a vase was on the tray along with a sealed manila envelope. I'll never forget his words, "I'm so sorry, baby. Eat your breakfast first and then open the envelope." Then he left the room.

My jaw hurt, but I was able to eat a little bit. I opened the envelope and there were over a hundred photos of me in various sexual positions with numerous men and a note that said, "I have more copies to send to the school, post on social media, and to send *to your proud parents. You can't go to the police because they are in my back pocket, just like you are now. So get over it. You are mine to do with as I please. Oh, and there was some property taken from the mansion that has been reported missing and the owners have your information, fingerprints, and the items have been strategically placed so the police, with a search warrant, can find them and that means prison, baby."*

ANN KIDWELL

Chapter Forty-Eight
Alex

I arrived at the station and got the numbers for Sue and Sabrina's parents. The records clerk had pulled the missing person sheets on each of them. They had been missing more than two weeks. Even in that short period of time, I knew that their lives had been changed forever. I directed my staff to put the parents in two separate rooms when they arrived.

I wanted to fill them in on what to expect from their daughters. This would be a very difficult time for them but at least they had been found alive and safe. "Call the YWCA and find a victim's advocate to talk with each set of the parents with information on outreach programs. We need to get the girls fed and feeling safe first. There will be a lot of questions coming at them from their parents and from us."

Officer Bunch approached, "Sue Kingston's parents are in interrogation room one and Sabrina Moore's parents are in interrogation room two."

"Thank you, officer. Would you please check with the Moore's to see if they would like some coffee and let them know that I'll be in to see them in about twenty minutes? Have Sandy meet me in interrogation room one."

I watched the Kingston's through the security glass and saw that Mrs. Kingston was in business attire and was rubbing her eyes with a tissue. Her husband was hovering over her in a protective manner. I could tell that they had been through hell. I knocked on the door and then opened it. "Good morning, Mr. and Mrs. Kingston. My name is Detective Alexandra Prosser. Would you like some coffee or something to drink?"

"No, we're just anxious to see Susie," Mr. Kingston said.

"Yes, of course, I understand. Your daughter Susie was found this morning and is, at this moment, finishing her pancakes. I won't take up much of your time because I know you want to see her. I just wanted to let you know a little bit about what Susie has gone through before you see her. Have either of you heard of human trafficking?"

"Oh, no, oh, God," Mrs. Kingston cried as her husband reached over to comfort his wife.

"I'm sorry to tell you that we believe she was abducted by traffickers. She seems to be doing okay physically at the moment, but emotionally she has been through a lot. That's why I have an advocate here to fill you in on what that means." I handed a box of tissues to Mr. Kingston. "I am so sorry this has happened to your family, but hopefully we can help you get through this."

Mrs. Rogers has worked with a lot of human trafficking victims and can explain to you more of what to expect. So, if you have any questions now or if you think of some when you get home, here are our cards. Feel free to contact us. In about ten minutes, I'll have you taken to where your daughter is, I just wanted to prepare you; she will need your ongoing support.

"Have you arrested the animals that did this to my daughter?" Mr. Kingston asked with clinched fists while pacing the room.

"No, we haven't as of yet but we have some strong leads we are following up. I will keep you updated as our investigation progresses."

I left room one and headed into room two to tell Mr. and Mrs. Moore the same thing about Sabrina.

Once the girls had been united with their parents, I got permission to ask the girls a few questions before they went home and then follow up with more detailed questions later.

I addressed the girls. "When we found you at the cabin today, you were alone and it appeared that a snowmobile had left about two hours before we rescued you. How many people were at the house with you? Do you know their names? Sabrina, you said by your watch, Mandy left on the snowmobile around six o'clock in the morning and that Keilan went to the Super Bowl. Is that correct?"

Sabrina nodded her head. "Mandy said we worked for Keilan now. He owns us. He bought us from another pimp. But he was gone when we got there.

"Just a couple more questions. Do you know Mandy's last name?"

Sabrina and Susie both shook their heads no.

"Two more questions, then you can go home. Do you remember any place that Mandy would have gone or anyone that she may have called?"

Susie jumped in and said, "Last night Mandy took us with her to see her boyfriend and told us not to tell Keilan and she would get us a treat. It was at 610 McDonald. I have a thing for numbers and I like McDonald's. But that's all I know. Oh yeah, and she called him Freddy. Does that help?" she beamed.

"Oh, sweetie, that helps a whole bunch. Why don't you go home with your parents and get some rest." Alex looked at the Kingston's and the Moore's and said, "Thank you for letting me ask them the questions. The clerk at the desk will schedule a time for you to come back and speak with me. I will have some follow-up questions when we get more into the case. If the girls remember anything else, feel free to call me. I look forward to seeing you again soon." I shook hands with the parents and the little girls. I said "You have been so brave Thank you for your help." I escorted them to the clerk's desk.

ANN KIDWELL

Chapter Forty-Nine
Alex

The officers that were left at the cabin followed the snowmobile tracks until they meshed with all the other tracks at the ski lodge. There was a video camera at the lodge. The task force checked the video for signs of anyone matching Mandy's description but they were unsuccessful in finding her. Most of the skiers had on snowsuits or knit stocking caps. They did find an unclaimed snowmobile that they assumed was the one she had driven.

They had video footage of cars coming and going from the lodge and hoped to find one that left with more passengers than they had come with. Combing through the videos with the snowmobiles and cars was a long and arduous task but they were close. We had all put in late hours but around 10 p.m. they had to stop and pick it up in the morning.

The next morning, bright and early, we were back at it. "I want you to check every 610 McDonald Avenue, Street, Lane, loop and any other McDonald that you can find. Check all cities in this vicinity, especially, if there is a Fred or Freddy or Frederick listed there, then get back to me. We are getting closer, I can feel it. That's all we have to go on at this time and I don't want Mandy to get away, so if you have any ideas, I'm listening."

Within twenty minutes, they got a hit on 610 McDonald in Edmonds. A Freddy Adcock was the tenant and he had water and electric in his name at that address.

I asked the records clerk to check the databases to see if he had any vehicles registered in his name and cross reference that with plates from the ski lodge videos to see if there are any matches.

I had just gotten a second cup of coffee and was making my way back to my desk when they got the match we were looking for. That match was enough for a search warrant and an arrest warrant for Mandy or Amanda Doe.

An hour later, armed with the warrants, we surround the residence of 610 McDonald and knocked on the door.

"Who is it?" A man asked.

"Lynnwood Police Department."

A rustling sound filled the air, a back door opened and Mandy ran right into the arms of the officer waiting there.

"Mandy Doe, you are under arrest in an investigation of kidnapping and human trafficking of minors Sue Kingston and Sabrina Moore." Her rights were read, and she was put in the police cruiser for transport to the Lynnwood Police Department.

Based on an expired driver's license found on Mandy, they were able to get her full name, Amanda Baker. A missing person's report had been filed on her over three years ago by her parents when she didn't come home from college. She had escaped detection since her disappearance. She had been placed in interrogation room one and was left to stew while I planned a strategy for questioning her. Grabbing a notepad, I stepped into the room.

"I know that you're just a pawn in this human trafficking case and we know the primary person is Keilan Angelino. Any information you can give in helping us to apprehend Keilan will go in your favor."

"I'm not stupid. I'm not saying a thing until my attorney gets here." Mandy glared at Alex.

At that I shook my head. "Book Amanda Baker on the charges of two counts of kidnapping and two counts of trafficking of a minor for purposes of rape with reference to Sue Kingston and Sabrina Moore. That's just the beginning." Alex turned toward Mandy and continued, "We will be adding the charges with reference to Connie Young and Tina Miller. You can bet we will be bringing in Keilan soon, so you will need to get ahead of this or you'll be spending life in prison. I hope Keilan is worth it."

I left the interrogation room and headed to the Snohomish County Prosecutor's Office to speak with the prosecutor with reference to the case. From there I headed home for a much needed rest.

Chapter Fifty
Becca

We were on our way to San Francisco and excited that we get to have a break from being stuck in that room and having to work. Keilan had said that he would give us more liberties but that we better not cross him or he would kill us and bury us along the way.

I sat in the front with Keilan, since I was "his favorite" as the other girls said. But I believe it is because I have earned his trust by keeping my promise not to try and run away after he let Tina go. He thinks I help to keep the other girls in line, but that isn't so. I have built a trust with the other girls, that I will have their back. Jessica has grown sullen and bitter and I understand that. I tried to give her some hope, but she long since quit believing in the happily-ever-afters or any fairy tales for that matter. I've found that if I give her some space, Jessica will come around.

Jessica and Penny were in the backseat playing a game called "slug-bug" where every time a player spots a Volkswagen Bug they got to slug the other player in the arm. They loved gawking at the scenery and were awed at some of the cars on the highway. They made silly faces at little children in cars that passed by since they knew the tinted windows keep people from seeing in. It's the most relaxed we've been in a long time. It had been nearly six months since I had run away. I haven't given up hope yet. Hope that I would get to go home soon. The dreams of the Indian girl and the white owl gave me hope and that is all I had to hold onto at this time.

Penny and I had become close—the two most unlikely of friends. We formed a bond of trust and I had told her about my dreams of the owl and the Indian girl. Penny wasn't sure if she believed me, but she hadn't laughed when I'd told her. At night we pretend to sleep but whispered for hours. We are keeping our bond a secret; otherwise, Keilan would try to separate us.

Together we have devised a plan of escape and were hoping to pull it off when we got to San Francisco. We felt the area would be more populated, so easier to get help. But for now, we are going to enjoy this little bit of rest.

Chapter Fifty-One
Becca

I still had dreams once in a while about the big white owl and the Indian girl. The dreams used to come more frequently but haven't much lately. I hope every night when I lie down from exhaustion that I will dream of the Indian girl and the beautiful white owl, Casper. The dreams kept me from feeling so alone.

The Indian Girl had told me that her name was Nunnehi and that she was from the Cherokee Wolf Clan. She called the white owl Casper because he was a ghost or spirit animal. She said that he was her eyes and he is there to help me. She said that I cannot tell anyone about my dreams, unless I really trust them.

I try to sleep longer because I want to escape from the realities of the situation I'm in.

Why didn't I listen to Connie? God, I hope she made it home safe. The Indian girl said she had. Connie had taught me a very important lesson and that was to listen to my instincts. She had said that something wasn't right and she had been right. In the back of my mind I knew it was too good to be true. But I had pushed my doubts away because I didn't want to believe anything bad about Keilan. I had been so wrong. I don't know how many times I've wished I could take back all the fights with Mom and Sissy. My life had been so easy now that I look back on it. All Mom had wanted was for me to go to school and learn and do a few chores around the house like keeping my room clean. Oh, what I wouldn't give to be back in my room.

No one could have made me believe that this is what would happen to my life. I never dreamed that I would be a prostitute. How many times had I been told you shouldn't ever meet up with someone you met online, that it could be dangerous? I didn't believe them. I thought they were just trying to run my life. I was so wrong. Thinking I was mature and not trusting or listening to my Mom had gotten me into this mess.

In my last dream, Nunnehi had told me she was going to let me see what was going to happen in my future. She let me see through Casper's eyes. He was high in the sky and looked down on a big stadium with large parking lots around it. I assumed that was where the Super Bowl would take place. During the dreams, Nunnehi can speak to me. I cannot speak to her I can only nod my head yes or no. This dream gave me hope that someone knows where I'm going. The dreams feel so real I hope they are real.

We stopped at a motel about 20 miles off the highway. Just to be on the safe side Keilan had said. We stayed in a room with two king-sized beds and a rollaway bed. Penny and I slept in one of the king-sized beds and Keilan slept in the other. Jessica slept on the rollaway. It was a small Mom and Pop style motel but it was clean. Keilan didn't have any interest in young girls except for what he could make off them on their backs. He spent a lot of time playing video games and turned his phone off because he just wanted to chill. We were able to watch the TV and chat.

At one point when Keilan went into the bathroom, Penny asked me if we were still going to go through with it. I nodded yes, and showed her the little container I had in my purse. We both smiled and went back to watching TV.

Chapter Fifty-Two
__Becca__

I was shaken awake by Keilan.

"Come on, get up. We need to get an early start. I want to get there before it gets dark. Get your showers and do your hair. I have a welcome party for you when we get there. Don't take too long or you will have to skip breakfast."

I had had another dream last night. I saw Casper flying over the freeway, then I saw the Indian girl. Nunnehi had spoken to me. "We know that you are somewhere along Interstate 5 in Oregon but haven't been able to get an exact location. We do know that you are headed to San Francisco for the Super Bowl, so be patient. Please don't do anything that would jeopardize your life or the lives of the two girls that are with you. Just know that we are getting closer. I can only see what Casper sees from great distances and I can see what you look like but cannot see your mouth move so I can't read your lips. Casper is our best chance of finding you and I don't want you to lose hope. Casper will be going dark so this will be the last chance I get to talk to you until you sleep again. Hopefully, he will be able to pick up your trail."

I remembered all the details of the dream and it gave me hope. I couldn't share any of that with Penny because we were never alone. It was probably for the best because I wasn't certain it wouldn't accidentally slip out. It was making me anxious though. After eating breakfast, I watched through the car windows once we were back on the interstate looking for any sign of Casper.

Nunnehi, what a pretty name. It even sounds Indian.

I said a silent prayer that I had repeated numerous times throughout the last six months. It was a children's prayer I had learned when I was young, but I added more verses.

Now I lay me down to sleep,
I pray the Lord my soul to keep.
If I should die before I wake,
I pray the Lord my soul to take.

I know the tears my momma cries for me

Please bring her comfort and relief.
Whisper that I miss her so
And send my love that she will know,
To keep me in her prayers at night,
For God will make all things right.

Carry me home on silver wings,
While a chorus of Angels sing,
For peace and love to wipe out sin
And the world's children will be safe again.

We entered California and I spotted Casper on the overhead sign when we exited onto Highway 280. We traveled on this highway for a while then turned south on Highway 17 to Los Gatos and I saw Casper again. I hoped that he was able to keep track of us. Then we made another turn down a road and pulled up outside a beautiful mansion.

Chapter Fifty-Three
Nunnehi

"Alex, I need you to come to my house as soon as you can. I'm receiving clues from Casper and I see the Lexus on Highway 5 in California. I think I'm seeing in real time and I think Casper is following them. Please, hurry." I hung up to focus on what I was seeing. Alex arrived and was relaying, by phone, what I was seeing to the ground commander with Operation Web Weaver Task Force in San Francisco.

"Casper is showing me Highway 280."

Alex gave the information to the ground commander and they now had a visual on the silver Lexus. They were following the Lexus at a safe distance. Finding the location of the residence where the traffickers are set up to meet and not jeopardizing the safety of the girls was paramount. This was believed to be the primary location of one of the Super Bowl gatherings. They were maintaining a visual at all times, changing the tracking car frequently.

Casper showed me Becca watching out the window as they turned on Highway 17 to Los Gatos. She appeared to be looking at Casper. They turned right and pulled up outside of a large mansion. It's bigger than any house I've ever seen. Casper is real close to the car, and I can see in the front window which isn't tinted of the Lexus and Becca nodding to a girl in the backseat. I'm surprised that I can hear Keilan's voice when I hadn't been able to hear anyone before.

"Well, ladies we are here and you are about to make me a very rich man. Get your shit together. They are expecting you so we mustn't keep them waiting." With that, he put the Lexus in park and turned the key in the ignition off. Instantly, Becca grabbed the keys and opened her door, as did the girl in the back. At the same time, the girl with orange hair grabbed the other girl's arm and pulled her through the backdoor. The girls exited the vehicle and Becca threw an open container at Keilan. They slammed the door shut and Becca pushed the lock button on the key fob. Keilan was trapped in the car. Becca grabbed Jessica's free hand and the girls were in a dead run down the block and ran right into two police cars with lights flashing. More patrol cars arrive, blocking the street.

They stopped and an officer came up to them. "You don't need to run anymore. You're safe now." At first, Becca thought they are going to arrest her and the girls for prostitution. Then the officer's words ran through her head. "You're safe now." She crumbled to the ground with uncontrollable sobbing. All three girls cry huddled together.

A female officer leads them to a more secure area and Becca hears a noise. Casper is on a street sign. Becca nods toward the owl and whispered, "Thank you."

The commander relayed to Alex that the girls were safe. Alex let the commander go and I continued to give Alex the play by play as I saw it.

I cried with relief. I could hardly catch my breath through my sobs. "They…oh, God, they're safe" The tears flow down my cheeks and I hugged Alex. I can't stop shaking. "Oh my, God, Becca is safe."

Alex wrapped me in her arms and cried with me. "We never could have done this without your help. You'll be okay, Nunnehi. You will be okay, you beautiful graceful warrior." She whispered as she held me tight.

***

Alex

It was my turn to fill in Nunnehi as to what was being relayed to me over the radio. The officers surrounded the Lexus. The SWAT team entered the residence. Guns were drawn on Keilan and when they order him to get out of the car, they notice a look of terror on his face. He was being observed by an officer through the front windshield as the tint on the other windows was too dark. They could hear him screaming for help.

"Let me out of here! I'm going to die! No… no… no, I can't get away no…no…no…no…no! Let me out of here! I'm going to die…" He was trying to get the door open and beat on the window of the car.

The guns were trained on him and the police were ready to break the window out, when an officer hurried around the corner, clicked the remote, and the doors unlatched.

Keilan jerked on the door handle and when it opened he tumbled out of the car, screaming in agony and scratching at his face and shirt. He continued to scream and pleaded with them for help. He fell over on his side and appeared to be having a seizure.

The officer with the keys walked up. "Here's the keys. One of the girls jerked them out of the ignition and locked him in the vehicle.

Apparently, you can't get out of the car when it's locked with this key fob."

The joint task force and local officers assisted Keilan and called for an ambulance. He was frothing at the mouth and his eyes were rolled back in his head. He was incoherent, and didn't respond to verbal commands. They roll him over and removed the gun from the back of his waistband. He was put on a stretcher and an officer boarded the ambulance with him.

As they were loading him into the ambulance, a lady that appeared to be in her early 50's rushed up to him, yelling. "Keilan?" "What have you done to my son?" She pushed her way past the police as they tried to stop her.

Keilan appeared to have responded to her voice, then lapsed back in to unconsciousness.

"I will have your badges for this." She tried pulling free from their grasp. "You have no right to be here, this is my house." She began yanking her arms free. It took two officers to subdue the struggling woman. She was handcuffed and put in the back of a patrol car.

One of the officers noticed a bunch of Wolf Spiders where Keilan laid on the ground. He grabbed a paper napkin from the inside of the car and picked up one of the spiders. "They can have a nasty bite, but usually not deadly." He said as he gave his captured spider to the officer in the ambulance. "You may want to let the doctor know that he was probably bitten by several of these." The EMT handed him a specimen container to put the spider in.

The task force officer told Alex, "The girls were taken to the hospital to be checked out. I'll call and update you when we know more."

ANN KIDWELL

Chapter Fifty-Four
__Alex__

Before I boarded a plane bound for San Francisco, I contacted Nunnehi, promising to call her when I got back to Washington so we could tie up the loose ends on this operation.

I volunteered to pick up the girls from the shelter the next morning and drive them back to Lynnwood. The girls had been allowed to call their parents and would meet them at the Lynnwood Police Station. Corresponding arrests had been made across the country and the mansion in Los Gatos garnered twelve more rescued minors and the apprehension of seven traffickers. They still hadn't gotten the master of the operation, Weaver, but they were getting close.

Penny's foster parents were contacted but they had not reported the girl as missing. The authorities were working to get an emergency shelter for her when they returned to Washington.

Becca, Jessica, and Penny met me when I picked them up from the YWCA. Becca was surprised that I knew so much about her.

I explained that I'd spoken to Connie right after she had gotten away. That Connie had hidden in a truck at the rest area and called for help when she got to a restaurant. Becca was so glad that Connie was all right.

Becca talked out loud to herself. "Maybe I'm all wrong. Maybe praying to God that someone would come and help me, just had me seeing what I wanted to see. That doesn't explain the owl? I saw the owl. The white owl everywhere I went, but no one else saw it."

On the trip back to Washington I told Becca, "That was a brave thing you did, helping to save Tina. She told us how you fought to get Keilan to take her to the hospital. She was very close to dying. You saved her life."

Becca cried. "I couldn't let her die, I just couldn't." she said through her tears.

Jessica said, "Becca took care of all of us. She fought for us. She would put herself between Tina and Keilan. What's going to happen to Keilan?" she asked.

"As far as I know, he's still in the hospital, in a psych ward. He can't get out. He hasn't been coherent enough to question yet. Whose idea was it to lock him in the car with spiders? That was ingenious."

Penny spoke up. "I had a thing for spiders in biology and when Becca told me that he was afraid of spiders, I knew that I wanted him to experience the fear we experienced. At night, Becca and I would plot and plan. We had to work it when we'd both be in the car at the same time. When he told us we were going to San Francisco, we collected them the morning we left. We hoped we could keep them alive. Neither of us could believe that it went as smoothly as it did."

Becca asked, "Is it true that we aren't going to be charged with prostitution? We didn't want to do it, Keilan made us. He told me that he would kill my sister and mother. He showed me their pictures, and he knew where they were. He took pictures when they were at the park and he had a picture of my house and Sissy with Barney, our St. Bernard. I just couldn't let him kill my family. At least he can't get to them now and they'll be safe."

"No, Becca, none of you will be charged with prostitution. None of you wanted to do what you were forced to do. We know that. So rest, it will be awhile before we're home."

After a bit, the three girls fell asleep in the car. When we got back to the police department, Jessica's family was waiting for her and Becca's mother would arrive the following day. Becca and Penny would stay at the YWCA Women's Shelter for tonight. There would be a counselor for them to talk to. It was after midnight when we get back to Lynnwood and it has been an exhausting day for me, but I felt a rush of adrenaline. I'm not sure if I will be able to sleep or not. I felt a warm glow inside.

This is what matters. This is why I do this job.

Chapter Fifty-Five
Alex

I checked on the status of Keilan, and he is still at a mental facility in San Francisco. He had not come out of the catatonic state he was in. The doctor said he was in shock and assumed that he had a severe case of Arachnophobia. The doctor said that if he had had a bad heart, it would have killed him. He was not sure when he would come out of it. They would wait and see.

I learned through the task force that Keilan's mother, Barbara Angelino, was the infamous "Weaver." Through questioning of a guy named Michael Mason, it was disclosed that Keilan did not know that his mother was the head of the organization and that she had planned to tell him when he arrived. *Oh, the webs we weave.* I thought to myself.

The next morning I stopped by Nunnehi's on my way to the YWCA to pick up Becca and Penny. I had sent a detective to pick up Becca's mother at the airport. They would meet us at the police station.

I knew this could not have been accomplished without the assistance of Nunnehi—Skye. I've developed a great fondness for her. I'm still not sure about her "gift," but it was a pivotal part in the rescue.

Nunnehi asked me to call her Skye when she wasn't channeling Casper. She had sounded anxious when I called to see if she wanted to meet Becca. Shyness upon meeting someone new still plagued her. But she said she felt such closeness to Becca, she wanted to talk to her and see for herself that she was safe.

When Skye met her at the YMCA, Becca ran to her. "You are real, you are really real." The tears ran down her cheeks and she hugged Skye.

Skye hugged her back and said, "I'm so sorry this has happened to you. From the time I saw you at the airport, we connected, but I didn't know how until much later. I'm sorry that I couldn't have saved you before now. Please, forgive me."

Becca hugged her. "You saved my life. I don't know how you were able to walk and talk in my dreams. I thought you were an angel, but you're flesh and bone. I also saw a white owl. Do you have a white owl?"

Skye smiled and said, "Yes, I do. He's my spirit guide. He led me to you. I don't think I would tell anyone though, because they may not believe you. Let's keep this our secret. Only someone special like you can see him. Deal?" Skye asked Becca.

"Deal," Becca said. She noticed the earphones that Skye had around her neck. "What kind of music do you listen to?"

Chapter Fifty-Six
<u>Alex</u>

I sat down to type up my report and to tie-up some loose ends to close out our side of Operation Web Weaver.

All total, the joint task force across numerous states and venues had apprehended 94 traffickers, and 111 children were saved in one of the biggest sting operations in the US. As calls are being received, more leads are being followed.

U.S. Prosecutor Donald Timothy came to give the detectives an update on another matter they were pursuing in the case.

"We have been speaking with Mandy Baker and her attorney. She is willing to give us the head of the operation. She said that not even Keilan knew who the head of the operation was, and she found out purely by accident. She kept it to herself because she thought it might come in useful if she ever got in the situation that she's in now. It appears she was a little late in playing that card."

I told Mr. Timothy, "We have been unable to question Keilan. He's been unconscious since they found him locked in the Lexus." She shook her head. "I can't believe the plan that Becca and Penny executed to getting away. That just blows my mind. How did they think of something like that? Wolf spiders? Wow! Just wow."

Mr. Timothy agreed and shook his head. "That's one for the books, and surprising enough, Becca and Penny are both great and credible witnesses.

"Leads keep coming in and Mandy was involved with personally trafficking at least ten victims. We are still interviewing victims. From some of the information we have gleaned, she took her orders from Keilan. It appears she started out as a victim herself, but ended up a key player long after she could have gotten out. But that is for the professionals to ascertain as to whether she was a willing participant or not," Alex said to the prosecutor.

"Okay, keep me in the loop. I'll need more information on where you're getting your leads. You just listed that the information came from a CI. Can you tell me anymore about who that was?" Mr. Timothy asked.

"Well, not at this point but I'll give you more information as I complete my report."

"Okay, great job, Alex. This wouldn't have happened without the information we received from your department. Now get some much needed rest." Mr. Timothy left the office.

Alex grabbed her coat and scarf as she headed out the door. "I'm heading to a nice bottle of Chardonnay with a handsome blue-eyed Cherokee and I'm forwarding my calls to voicemail. See you on Monday."

HUMAN TRAFFICKING RESOURCES/ADVOCATES

The Polaris Project - NHTRC (National Human Trafficking Resource Center) 1-888-373-7888 was instrumental in Connie's rescue. SOAP - Save Our Adolescence from Prostitution

O.U.R. – Operation Underground Railroad – Founded December 2013

(W)e've gathered the world's experts in extraction operations and in anti-child trafficking efforts to bring an end to child slavery. O.U.R.'s Underground Jump Team consists of former CIA, Navy SEALs, and Special Ops operatives that lead coordinated identification and extraction efforts. These operations are always in conjunction with law enforcement throughout the world.

Once victims are rescued, a comprehensive process involving justice for the perpetrators and recovery and rehabilitation for the survivors begins.

It is time for private citizens and organizations to rise up and help. It is our duty as a free and blessed people.

Domestic Services
O.U.R. salutes our nation's law enforcement officers and prosecutors at the federal, state and local levels who protect our country's children. Law enforcement professionals skillfully investigate, arrest and prosecute those who violate children. Our nation's police efforts to protect children in the U.S. are light years ahead of many, if not all other countries. O.U.R. acknowledges the expertise and extraordinary work done by these dedicated men and women who bravely battle the scourge of child sexual exploitation. O.U.R. shares the mission to save children and seek justice for those who victimize them, therefore O.U.R. is committed to enhancing law enforcement efforts by providing resources where budget shortfalls prohibit a child pornography, child exploitation or human trafficking operation from going forward. O.U.R. will also provide or facilitate child exploitation investigative training in U.S. jurisdictions where a need exists. Collaborating with law enforcement will reduce duplication, promote best practices and avoid other potential issues which might arise without close coordination. O.U.R. is privileged and honored to support our nation's heroes in this important cause to deter, disrupt and dismantle child

exploitation and the trafficking of children in our nation's communities.

Copied from O.U.R. Website

The S.O.A.P Project – Soapproject.org – 614-216-1619 – P.O. Box 645, Worthington OH 43085 "Save Our Adolescents from Prostitution"

S.O.A.P. was created to not only educate and save, but also to fill a need. After founder Theresa Flores would speak to a group of people at awareness events, she noticed the attendees were in shock, frustrated and yes, even angry. They demanded to know what they could do to stop this crime and protect their children.

S.O.A.P. allows concerned citizens to help put a stop to human trafficking in their community and save missing children. Kids as young as 9 years old, fathers with their sons, and an 83 year old nun have put labels on bars of soap. There *is* something you can do about this! The beauty of S.O.A.P. is that it is simple and easy and can be customized to your wants, needs and abilities.

Results

How do we know this works?

We get this question a lot. For a few years, our normal response had been, "We don't know. We just have faith that it does." However, that answer has recently changed.

- 83-100% of all hotels accept the labeled soap during an outreach.
- Almost 100% of the hotels take the missing children poster and trafficking educational materials.
- Generally at least 1 missing child is identified by hotel staff during each outreach.
- Polaris Project has reported that calls double to the hotline number the week S.O.A.P. has done an outreach.

- Michigan Crimes Against Children agency reports a dramatic increase in calls to their tip line during outreaches.
- Each outreach consists of 30-500 volunteers. Once volunteers have completed the outreach, they are now educated in Human Trafficking 101.
- Each hotel receives $50 worth of free materials and resources.

Testimonials

Some things might not have a measurable goal. And it really doesn't matter how many are saved. One is enough. All that really matters is that we are doing something about this issue.

Amanda

Name has been changed

Theresa was sitting in a small group setting at a local drug and alcohol residential recovery program for women and sharing her story. She was asked by one of the ladies about S.O.A.P. and how we knew it works. She gave her normal response and then a woman in the circle spoke out quietly, "My name is Amanda and I know it works!" Theresa thought she was just being nice and supportive but the woman continued on, "Four months ago I was in a Detroit motel near the airport and the 'John' started to go crazy on me. He was high and beat me and I was scared for my life so I ran into the bathroom with my cell phone and locked the door. I saw a bar of soap with a red label and called the number on it. The police rescued me and I got into a recovery program and here I am today. Thank you. It saved my life."

Stephanie

Name has been changed

A group of women in New Hampshire have been doing regular outreaches for the last few years. At church one Sunday, they announced an upcoming S.O.A.P. outreach and human trafficking awareness event. Stephanie came up to their table after church and asked for more information. She revealed to them that she was a survivor and just recently had gotten free. "I have seen the bars of soap in the motels! Some of the pimps (traffickers) are now going into the rooms with the girls so its hard to call but us girls on the streets have been talking about it and know it's there. Even if we can't call, it's so wonderful to know that there are people out there that care and are doing this!"

Columbus, Ohio

During an annual outreach, a team went into a small hotel and showed the front desk clerk the missing children poster. The woman started to cry. She said, "That is my niece's picture. I didn't think anyone cared or was looking for her. Thank you."

During another outreach, a team went to a low end motel in a high risk part of town. Before they got out of the car, they noticed an older white man in his late 50's going into a motel room with a young African American girl, approximately 15 years old, with a lot of make up on and looking down to the ground. The police were immediately notified.

Detroit, Michigan

A team of women from the Birmingham Junior League returned for the second year to go out to hotels and were discussing in the car that they were a little frustrated that they hadn't heard of any result or indication this really worked. They asked to go to the same hotels as the previous year and on their first stop, they went in and the manager was very happy to see them. He greeted them and said, "Oh, you're here with more soap! Did you know a girl was rescued last year after you left?" Within a few days, he had recognized a missing child on the poster and called the police. She was recovered that night. The team left there with huge smiles, energized to do even more.

Phoenix, AZ Super Bowl 2015

A team came back and reported that a hotel staff recognized a 15-year-old from the poster. They said that she had been there that night with her "Boyfriend" The police were notified and went to the hotel, where they got the male's information. Later that day he was arrested and she was recovered, along with another 15-year-old girl. Apparently they had been searching for this big time pimp for a while!

(*Copied from the* ***S.O.A.P. Project*** *website*)

NCOSE - National Center on Sexual Exploitation - 440 1ˢᵗ Street NW, Suite 840, Washington DC 20001, 202.393.7245, PUBLIC@NCOSE.COM

INK 180 - Covering or Removing Sex Trafficking Brands - Mission: I want to help former gang members and the survivors of sex trafficking re-enter society and move forward from their old lifestyle. Nobody should have to look at the marks that once labeled them. We're all about people getting a second chance and helping them to do so by covering or removing the old, painful reminders of a time gone by. Call (630)554-1404 Chicago.

THORN (Thorns protect the Rose) – Donate to Wear Thorn www.wearthorn.org – Thorn builds technology to defend children from sexual abuse.

WARN – Washington Anti-Trafficking Response Network 206-245-0782

Alameda County H.E.A.T. Watch Tip Line: 1-510-208-4959
Office of the District Attorney, Alameda County
Nancy E. O'Malley, District Attorney

SAS – Seattle Against Slavery - 3233 NW 61st St, Seattle, WA 98107 · (360) 747-7231

Though this is a fictional story, Human Trafficking is very real and is taking place in almost every city in the United States. Educate yourself on what the signs are, as you may save a life and help bring our children home.

ANN KIDWELL

ABOUT THE AUTHOR

This is my first try at writing a novel. I chose this subject as I felt there was a message that I needed to get out there and I wanted to deliver it in a way that would be interesting to young adults and anyone else that liked paranormal stories. The Cherokee Spirit Animal aspect is a subject that has always been of interest to me. I really enjoyed the research involved in the naming ceremony and also in the vision quest.

I believe that we all possess gifts that we can use to better the lives of mankind. The lesson that I hope I passed along in this story is that we are innately blessed with an intuition that has been honed through thousands of years of evolution and we need to trust those instincts. Just as Connie did. She felt that something wasn't right and therefore chose to try to escape from the situation. Too many times we don't trust what our bodies and minds are telling us, because what we want gets in the way. Stop – Pause and listen to your intuition.

I am a retired Paralegal and have a blended family. Yours, mine and ours which consist of a gnarly old husband I affectionately refer to a "Snap & Snarl," three sons – two-daughters -13 grandchildren – one senior mare – two gelded yearlings – one rough collie dog – two feral cats and one beautiful black rescue cat.

I look forward to writing book 2 – Aaron's story, so stay-tuned.

53553740R00138

Made in the USA
Columbia, SC
17 March 2019